Murder's Last Resort

Murder's Last Resort

by Marta Chausée

Oak Tree Press Taylorville, IL

Oak Tree Press books may be purchased for educational, business or sales promotional purposes. Contact Publisher for quantity discounts

First Edition, February 2013

ISBN 978-1-61009-049-0
LCCN 20122954595

To Opa and Mama,
who taught me about "Krimis"

Acknowledgements

Thank you to my loving mother, who taught me to read before I went to school and to my loving father, who modeled reading for information and pleasure every night of his life. Thank you to the storytellers of my childhood, Monika Dahl and Sharie Palm. Thank you to the ACN Laguna Beach Lushes, the Foothill Nightwriters, Sue Buckwell and Judy Kohnen. Thank you to my teachers Michael Harada, Richard C. Schwartz, Bruce McAllister, Syd Bartman and John Brantingham. Thank you to my editor, Sunny Frazier, my publisher, Billie Johnson, and to Alan Sacks. Thank you to my two sons, Cristian Robert Chausée Kelly and Brandon Tadhg Chausée Kelly, who have made my life worthwhile. Many thanks to the hospitality industry and those people in it I have loved. Without them, there would be no book.

Chapter 1

Redmund Torrey lay dead in his tuxedo in the middle of a huge pile of used white sheets and towels. When I ran into one of our maids, Maria, who had found Torrey and was screaming her head off in the laundry department, I did the right thing. I called security first, then French. I stayed with Maria and got her to pipe down, but I got about as much credit for that as a beggar at Lloyd's of London.

French, my husband, glared at me, his blue eyes frosty. "I still don't understand why you came back to the hotel."

"Like I told you, after we made love, I was energized. You know how I am. I couldn't sleep so I decided to visit Jake. He's on night audit. Is that such a crime?"

"No, but murder is," French snapped.

"Get real. You're not accusing me of murder?" I glared back at him, my blood starting to boil.

"No, but the Orlando PD will."

Not waiting for an answer, French turned on his heel, walked back to the corpse, and, hands in his pockets, stared. He could be so difficult at times. He didn't care what I had to say. I was just a further complication in what was going to be a doozy of a night.

French had arrived on scene in a lightning flash. We were waiting for our security guys, Bob and Dirk. I could hear their footsteps now, echoing like thundering rhinos in the cement block underground corridors of the hotel.

They rounded the corner and stopped short, drawing their guns and aiming at the laundry, as if the murderer might jump out from the pile of soiled and lumpy hotel linens. Following close behind them were David Enderly, French's property manager, and Lauren White, the PR gal. What was she doing here?

"Oh mah God," Lauren gushed, in her over-the-top Southern drawl. "What happened?"

French looked at her, said nothing, then looked at me. I got his message loud and clear. I was supposed to take charge of Lauren and keep her out of the men's way. The men would take care of this.

I obliged French because that was my job. A good hotel wife knew how to smooth over the most uncomfortable situations.

"Lauren," I said with a smile, "come here. Stand with Maria and me."

Her face registered her shock. She came over, but not until she had taken a good long gander at Torrey.

"Oh mah God," she said again, but this time her voice was hushed, a bit more collected. The pupils of her aqua eyes were as big as black holes in deep space. "Who would want Mr. Torrey dead?"

"Who knows?" I answered, though I had a few ideas rattling around my head. Torrey lived a bit too large. Had his wife been here, I would have suspected her. Then there were all the people he had managed to piss off in the hotel industry.

"Is he strangled?"

"Looks like."

Maria whimpered. I put my arm around her and she buried her face in my shoulder. I patted her back while I gave Lauren a look that said, "Cool it."

"Is that pantyhose around his neck?" Lauren whispered, her polished nails at her mouth.

"Yes, it is."

"It's tied in a bow, Maya," she said.

"I know. Creepy, isn't it?" I answered.

"Oh mah God," she said again.

She was as annoying and repetitious as a myna bird that knew only one phrase. She and the sobbing Maria were keeping me at the sidelines. I wanted to hear what French and the guys were saying.

"Lauren," I said, "calm down. The police will be here any minute."

Lauren smoothed the sides of her little black dress and stood, with the toes of her black patent high heels pointed slightly inward. With her long blonde hair, she looked innocent and sexy at the same time.

Just then, two of Orlando's finest arrived—Police Chief Rick Wells, and his chunky deputy, Detective Sergeant Tom Koenig.

The men clustered around Redmund Torrey. French explained to Rick and Tom that Torrey was the president of Sapphire Hotels and Resorts. He was still in his tux from the party we had all attended just a few hours earlier.

I tuned into their conversation as I stared at Torrey. Unlike gory messes I had walked in on in the past, this murder scene was surrealistic—so clean and white, except for Torrey's face already turning an unbecoming shade of purplish blue. His limbs were twisted into unnatural positions, as though he might be practicing an eerie Irish jig.

I felt sorry for him, poor fool. He wouldn't be addressing any more Manager's Conferences, no matter how prestigious or important they were.

Chapter 2

Rick and Tom came over and asked Maria what happened. She answered in Spanglish. We all got the gist. She had rolled one of the industrial baskets away from the hotel laundry chute and dumped its contents. As she loaded the washer, she unearthed a well-dressed gentleman, a crumpled heap of darks, amongst the usual tangle of hotel whites.

"I'm surprised to see you here," I said to Lauren.

"I stayed late after the party, Maya. I had to do a write-up about it for the *Sentinel*."

I looked at her and wondered. It was plausible.

"Mr. Enderly and I were going over a few things in his office when Mr. French's call came in," Lauren added.

I nodded. Had it been anyone else, I might have wondered about an office conference at such a late hour. But, Dave was a happily married man and Lauren was a nice southern girl. She dressed va-va-voomy, but she was straight-laced and conservative.

I wanted to talk with Police Chief Wells. I had some ideas I wanted to share with him. He was, of course, not at all interested in talking with me.

I saw my chance a few moments later. When Rick was done interviewing Maria, I caught his eye, nodded at Torrey and said, "I like the standard bow tie with tux combo better, don't you?"

"Not very funny, Mrs. French," Tom said, intercepting my comment to Rick. "Now's no time for jokes."

"Hey, I was talking to Rick, not you, pinhead." I wanted to tell Tom, but I kept my mouth shut. Both men didn't like me very much. Feelings mutual. I stole some of their thunder when I solved a weird, cold case murder at Church Lane Depot a few years ago. Ever since, they were offended that a little gal like me, an amateur, could produce results. In Tom's case, I had probably stepped on that bloated Southern male ego of his that matched his Florida gator belly.

Chapter 3

The stare Tom and Rick gave me made me uneasy. Surely they didn't think—?

"With all due respect, Mrs. French," Rick said, "what were you doing down here in the laundry area at 1:00 a.m.?"

"I couldn't sleep so I got up, got dressed and came to the hotel to chat with Jake. You know Jake Reynolds. We've been friends since eighth grade."

"Is that right, Mrs. French?" Rick said. He turned to Tom and said, "Make a note of that." Tom obligingly dug around under his belly for a notepad in his trouser pocket.

"I suppose Jake can verify that?" Rick continued.

"Of course. I left him just a few minutes ago. He's upstairs doing the night audit."

As Rick turned away from me, I could see him grinding his jaw. Tom looked up at me for a moment, then made another note in his little pad.

French came over, pulled me off to one side and said, "You see? It looks bad that you were in the hotel unsupervised."

"Unsupervised? What am I—a kid who's broken curfew?"

"No, you're my wife. It would be so nice if you started acting like it."

"What's that supposed to mean?"

"It means you should stay put, once we go home together."

"Well, you can always ground me," I said.

French shook his head, disgusted. "The point is, no one can verify where you were at the time of the murder."

"That's absurd. Jake can vouch for me."

"You think so?" he said. "I doubt he can cover you from the end of the party to the time you found Maria with Torrey. After all, I can't even do that and I was in bed with you."

I had no response. He was the judge and jury and I was in the wrong. I stood there, looking past him, feeling stupid. His disapproval was crushing.

He shifted gears, tilted his head toward Redmund and asked, "What do you think of this?"

Good riddance, was my first thought, because Torrey was not a good guy. On the other hand, no one deserved this. I covered my mixed emotions with a flippant, "It's a crime."

"Maya!" French looked exasperated.

"Okay. Here's what I think," I said, warming toward him for asking, "I think you'll discover the pantyhose is Size A. No woman invited to a Sapphire Manager's Conference wears hose larger than Size A."

I continued, "It's going to be support hose, too, because you need fibers strong enough to stop jiggling and cellulite if you're going to strangle someone to death with hosiery. This is an intimate crime, up close and personal, real hands-on, if you'll pardon the pun. Redmund knew his killer well and didn't suspect the attack."

Rick and Tom had been eavesdropping and now exchanged a look. They didn't like my opinions on a good day. Tonight they liked me and my opinions even less.

Just then, the medical examiner from Orlando arrived, along with the police photographer and other people in the CSI Department. It was getting crowded. Rick told us to stay nearby, so I walked back to Lauren and Maria. French went back to the guys. We hung around, awaiting for direction.

After some time on the hotel phone, Rick told us that, within fifteen minutes, the hotel would be surrounded by undercover cops. They would be everywhere—in both the public and the employee areas. They would be disguised as grounds people and housekeeping staff. They would be sweeping up imaginary leaves in the entry, parking lots, walkways and on the golf cart paths. They would be polishing brass knobs and elevator buttons.

Rick dismissed French, his staff and me but held Maria, the maid, for further questioning. Before he left for his office with Dave and Lauren in tow, French gave me a quick peck on the cheek and told me to be careful. The investigative team stayed with the body and began doing the things they do to keep evidence intact and to build a case.

If I thought I had been wide awake before, now I was wired with no hope of sleep. What was the point of going home alone? Instead, I asked Bob and Dirk to walk me through the back of the house, as we called the guts of the hotel, through the underground tunnels, to just under the ballroom. We keyed our way into the stairwell, past the ballroom and up into the main lobby.

In the lobby, we parted ways and I walked the travertine path beside the moss-covered streams, the fern-edged koi ponds and the empty parrot stands, past the elevated piano bar and the mirrored atrium elevators with their twinkling lights, all lined up in a row near the front desk.

I plunked myself down on one of the oversized, colonial rattan chairs near some hibiscus and palms. I sat in this empty pleasure dome at 3:00 a.m. and did some thinking. Who would want to kill Redmund Torrey? It was a puzzle, all right. How long could I make the list of suspects?

Chapter 4

I was sitting there, counting Torrey's bimbos and business associates, all of whom might have an axe to grind with him or some pantyhose to wrap around his silly goose neck, when I was startled by a noise right next to me.

"Geez Louise! You scared the hell out of me, you moron." I didn't mince my words and Jake looked stricken at my tone.

"Sorry, Maya. I didn't mean to startle you. I thought you heard me walk up. I was going back to the front desk from the safe. I saw some sandals I recognized, peeping out from behind the hibiscus. I just heard about Torrey from French and the gang," he said, sitting down next to me.

"Do you like these?" I asked him, raising and rotating my ankles in both directions so I could regard my sandaled little feet.

He looked down. "They are so Sesto, aren't they? Or are they Brunos?" Then, catching himself, he said, "Really, Maya. Do you think we should be admiring your shoes while there's probably a killer behind the next potted fern?"

I looked into his concerned blue eyes and nodded in agreement.

"Maya, who do you think did it?"

"It's a little too soon to tell," I said. "Torrey was disliked by so many people. He had almost unlimited power, he was the big boss man and a bit of a jerk—"

Jake interrupted me, "But he was also one of the old time greats—a little like Baron Hilton. All showmanship and the customer was king. You had to admire the guy."

"Maybe you did—"

Just then, there was a commotion off to the left. It was hard to see what was going on through the exotic flowers and foliage. Without conscious thought, we both popped out of our chairs and slunk down low, hiding behind the plants, like two kids watching adults through a bedroom window.

My eyes grew wide and my mouth gaped. We saw uniformed police moving someone toward the huge sliding glass entry doors of the hotel. The little group was making an exit to a waiting paddy wagon.

What the heck? I turned to Jake and asked, "Why are they leading French away in handcuffs?"

Chapter 5

Jake walked me across the property to my front door. "Do you want me to stay with you till morning?" he asked. "After all, it's almost morning already."

"No. Crazy as it sounds, I'm going to try to catch a few winks until I can call Doug."

"Doug? Doug Reed? He's still your attorney?"

"Yes, Jake," I answered with the patience I usually reserved for young children, "he's our attorney. We're all adults here and can let bygones be bygones."

"If you say so, Maya."

"I do, Jake. It's true."

"Okay, then I think you should call him now."

"Now? What for? Doug won't pick up his phone at 4:00 a.m."

Jake stared.

"Okay, Jake. I'll call his office. It'll go into voice mail. He'll hear from me as soon as he picks up his messages."

"That's better."

"I'm glad you're happy, Jake." I smiled. "Now, go back to work. Don't worry about me. The place is crawling with cops. Did you see the gardeners just outside my gates?"

Jake nodded.

"Not gardeners, but rather, disguised cops. Give me a hug and go."

He told me to lock my door. I watched him walk away.

Doug. I thought of him as I locked the glass-paneled, front doors behind me. Doug was a criminal attorney and a long-time personal friend who had once been a lover. He was damned good at all three things. Our transition from lovers to friends had not been drama-free. I could never understand how he could defend people he knew were guilty of committing a crime. He could never understand how I could leave him for the flake I dated before French. Over time, we had forgiven each other.

I walked into the bedroom—French's and my bedroom. A few hours ago, it had been our happy place, our private retreat from the hectic world in which we lived.

Normally, we faced our lives and the tourists that crawled in and out of every crevice and crack of the resort property together. We schmoozed VIPs at business dinners most nights of the week as a duo. We entertained and mingled with the owners of the Sapphire Corporation and the Norwegian property owners as a two-person team.

This particular week, it was the high energy, high stakes atmosphere of the 1985, week-long, once every five years, Sapphire Hotels and Resorts Manager's Conference. These gatherings were big deals because not only were the Sapphire owners there, but also owners of other hotel chains. They all assessed the various hotel managers and their wives. The impression a manager or his wife made at the conference could make or break his career in the entire industry, not just at Sapphire. A Sapphire conference was like pilot season or sweeps week on television. Some people got picked up, some people made the ratings and some got dropped from the lineup.

Now French was in cuffs and I was all alone. I walked over to our bed, peeled back my down-filled duvet and stretched out on my half of the bed.

Why had the police taken French? They were such boobs. Tears welled up but I choked them back and took a deep breath. What was the point of crying? It wouldn't help and it would give me a headache and puffy eyes. I had to put my feelings aside and rest, even if just for a short while. I tried some meditative breathing. "God, help French and me" on the inhale. "Make this all go away" on the exhale.

* * *

I caught almost five hours. I had been as limp as old celery left in the crisper too long when I went to bed. Now, I stretched and felt almost good. Then I remembered French. Then I remembered Torrey. Then I remembered Reed. My stomach felt sick.

It was a bright morning and the hotel was coming to life. From where I stood in my room, I could see the soft glow of the Central Florida sun, dancing on the sparkling blue lake beyond my deck. I made myself a cup of my morning tea—Darjeeling from Western Bengal.

Doug would get French out of jail post haste. Once this murder was cleared up and all our Sapphire guests had left, I could plan some away time with French. Western Bengal sounded good—distant enough to be an exotic adventure.

Now French was having an exotic adventure all his own in the downtown jail of Orlando. Or maybe not. He might be the only guy there. Orlando was not exactly known for its murderers, drug lords and rapists. Most crimes revolved around cigarettes stolen from the Circle K or people running red lights.

Orlando was better known for its two Ms, McDonnell Douglas and Mickey Mouse. McDonnell and Mickey had put Orlando on the map. Now French's behind was parked in the middle of that map in a cell on Orange Avenue.

I walked to the patio to drink my tea at the table. A blue heron swooped over me and I ducked. It perched on a nearby railing post. How long had we lived here now—over three years? I was still not used to the birds, the bugs and the reptiles.

Herons and egrets landed wherever they wanted, not at all spooked by humans. Snakes slithered away through the thick, leathery grass every time I walked from my front door to the hotel. The only Florida wildlife I liked was the playful otters that hung around the ponds between our property and Disney World. Most mornings, I encountered them as I walked the par course.

With the heron watching me, I picked up the phone, dialed Doug's number and started to tell him about French.

"Hi, Doug."

"Good morning, Maya," he said. "I'm already on it. I got your earlier message." His voice sounded smirky. He might find it funny that French was in jail, but it was no laughing matter to me.

"French will be out on bail in less time than it takes you to brew a pot of tea," he told me. "You still brew a lot of tea, don't you, Maya?"

"Yes, Doug. I still brew a lot of tea." I thought I best fill the silence with gratitude, so I continued, "Thanks for making French a priority."

We said our goodbyes and I did my morning rituals, thinking of French the whole time, and how I wanted to help speed along the solving of this case. I wasn't a policeman's daughter for nothing. My dad had been LAPD for over twenty years and retired. Then, he was a private investigator. Before his too-young death of a heart attack, he had shared his tales with my mom and me. I missed my Dad every day and—like father, like daughter, I guessed. Figuring out who done it was in my blood. Besides, what else was I doing? I wanted French here with me.

Chapter 6

I walked to the hotel along the volleyball beach and past the boat and windsurfer rental shack. Tots and their mommies were splashing in the kiddie pool. Oil-slathered sunbathers were already sucking up their Frangelico smoothies. Recreation department employees in their white polo shirts and shorts waved at me and said hello. All appeared in order on the happy, sunny playground of the Sapphire Silver Pines Orlando Resort. Our plum location next to Disney World kept us at a year-round 87% occupancy rate. We were always hopping.

I called Dave Enderly from a house phone on the lower level and he told me where to find the PD. He was letting them hole up in a small meeting room near the Grand Ballroom. This would be their makeshift, on-site office. I poked my head in the door and said hello to some of the guys.

French and I knew almost every policeman in Orlando, due to the frequent special events we hosted for the community. The guys were open with me. No results were back from the labs yet. No big news since last night. Where was Rick? I wanted to ask him why French was in jail. Did they really think he was involved in the murder?

Hubert French, my husband—everybody knew he was a people person, not a murderer. At employee Christmas parties, slightly tipsy maids from housekeeping asked him to dance.

Gardeners introduced him to their wives and families with pride. Kids from the rec department invited him to join them the next time they went hiking.

Who would ever suspect French of committing a murder? He was soft-hearted and fell for anybody's sob story, giving paid time off to anyone who said she or he needed it.

Me, I was not as popular as French. I was outspoken and un-swayed by fairy tales. Luckily, it was not my job to make judg-ments around the hotel or to hire or fire anyone. As a hotel wife, living on property, I was expected to be charming and gracious to all employees, guests and VIP visitors from around the world. Sometimes, my charm wore thin but I never quite ran out of it entirely. In the world of hospitality, it was all about pacing oneself while making nice-nice—then quick, carve out a little personal time to rest and regroup.

I said goodbye to the boys in blue in Meeting Room C and made my way upstairs to the hall behind the front desk. All the executive offices were bunched together there, and, since it was Saturday, the offices were dark. I thought I might run into little Pam, the executive secretary, but she wasn't in, either. I let my-self into French's locked office with my master key. Maybe there was something inside that he would want or need when I picked him up from jail in a little while. I looked around for his note pad and his pen. I found them and tucked them into my straw, summer bag. Something shiny in the top right corner of his desk, sticking out from among a stack of papers, caught my eye.

I pulled some computer read-outs and industry publications away from what turned out to be a receipt for some pantyhose, purchased at Walgreen's just yesterday, and a crushed silver, cardboard box with writing on its side: *L'eggs: They hug you, they hold you, they never let you go.* L'eggs, huh? Size B. Sun-tan. Of course, they were suntan. Ecru, ivory, taupe or beige would not have worked at a resort. But Size B? That was more surprising than a hippopotamus at a horse race.

Chapter 7

Huggins on Hiawassee was an old fashioned country road house—not the kind of place one would expect to see a Sapphire Resorts wife and her British friend, Lily, but that was exactly where we were. It was a hangout for Reedy Creek natives, the guys who draped the Rebel flag behind their gun racks in the back windows of their pick-up trucks. Their women were curvy with big hair. Lily and I were in jeans, t-shirts and cowboy boots. Not exactly down and dirty but not exactly posers, either. The idea was to disappear into the crowd.

We sat in a red leatherette booth, sipping our liquid lunches, a strawberry daiquiri for her and a banana daiquiri for me. The owner of Huggins, Kenny, knew us and was working the bar. He gave us extra melon balls and pineapple chunks. Lily was sliding fruit from a little plastic saber into her mouth, while I brought her up to date.

There had been a murder. French was accused and in jail. Doug was trying to get him out. Meanwhile, Rick, from the PD, had called to tell me that French wouldn't be released right away and he couldn't have visitors; there was no point in me driving to the city. Rick spoke with the indifference of someone reading a grocery list. I was about to lay into him when he also told me I was a person of interest and should stay on or near the hotel property at all times. I held my tongue, then immediately defied him and asked Lily to meet me at Huggins.

I told her about finding, grabbing and hiding the drug store receipt and pantyhose box I found in French's office. Probably no one would look for them at the bottom of a box of feminine products under my bathroom sink, which was where they were stashed now.

Finding the receipt and the pantyhose box had given me a flash of nausea. Why had they been on French's desk? He was always on higher moral ground than me. He could not commit murder, could he? I wanted French out of jail. I shredded my cocktail napkin into tiny squares and stabbed at them with my plastic saber, while I told all this to Lily.

Lily nodded. She let me finish, then said, "I can't believe Torrey's dead. He was such a big man—in so many ways..." She paused and I looked up.

"You didn't—" I said, examining her face and feeling just a little sick.

"Of course not. I'm only saying it was common knowledge...he had a lot to offer a girl."

"Oh now, that is just disgusting. Did you have to say that?"

"I'm sorry." She looked down, chastised for a moment, then went on, smiling. "He was quite the devil. The last time William and I attended an event, Torrey groped my bottom twice. He also touched me up on my left boob. A right nipple tweaker, he was."

I looked at her, picturing Red in his pantyhose neckwear. "Why does this not surprise me?" I asked.

"William didn't notice a thing, of course," she continued, matter-of-fact. "He was too busy prattling on about the Norwegian owners and the property. I managed to remove the tempting parts of my anatomy by gracefully sliding away from Red. He moved on to his next victim.

"Still, he had his charms, too," she said. "You had to stay a few feet away from him but he was fun. Was he his usual self the night he was killed?"

"Oh, sure, sure. Ever the alpha male, telling jokes, stroking the men's egos and stroking the ladies' thighs. All the while, he ignored his wife."

"That was him," Lily chimed in, "a true international grope. You know—Russian hands and Roman fingers."

"You got it!" I said. "Last night, he tricked me. Snuck up behind me right as he walked into the Munch Suite, where I stood, greeting all the bigwigs, including the Weinsteins, Sapphire's owners. Torrey's hand was under my skirt, on the back of my thigh, before I knew it. I slapped him away. He laughed and moved on. Later he cornered me in the kitchen. I wouldn't play along so he told me I was too flat. He gave me a handful of cocktail napkins and told me to stuff my bra. What an adolescent."

"Oh my," said Lily.

"He was such an ass! I would have loved to kill him myself. I sometimes fantasized about it," I said, my voice a little too loud.

"Mind yourself, Maya," Lily said, looking around to see if anyone had heard. "You can't say things like that now. You can't even think them."

"How about Alana?" I continued. "If Redmund were your husband, wouldn't you want to wring his neck just about every day?"

Lily contemplated this. "I think she rather enjoyed him. She loved the life he gave her. He did spoil her rotten, you said so yourself. In return, she looked the other way while he misbehaved. She must be devastated."

"I'm not even sure she knows yet. She left the party early last night headed for Atlanta, where her mother had surgery this morning."

"Hmm," said Lily. "Clever alibi, eh?"

"You said it," I answered. "Sorry to get back to French, but why do you suppose they won't let me go see him in jail? As soon as Rick told me French was staying there and could have no visitors, I called Reed."

"What did he say?" Lily asked.

"He said he's trying to get French out of jail but he ran into a snag. You don't think French could kill a man, do you?" My stomach gave a little lurch, while I waited for her answer.

"Even the finest of men can be provoked to murder," she said, drawing out the last word, for dramatic effect.

"Did I hear that right?" My eyes bugged out.

"Oh stop, Maya. Of course French didn't do the deed! You're being silly. There's probably a freak, hotel serial murderer on the loose—some little houseman or porter who came unhinged after spending too many years saying yes and amen to tourists. Someone else will be killed, French will still be locked up and that will pretty well put him in the clear, eh?" Lily said.

"That's a classic." I managed a grin. "A disgruntled former hotel employee. If you're right, postal workers will have to share the spotlight with them now."

"You get my point," she said, pleased with herself for making me smile.

"I certainly do." I felt like a fifty pound sack of coal had been lifted from my shoulders. It didn't show much heart for others, but the thought made me almost giddy. If something like that happened, my French would be in the clear.

Maybe talk of murder and the possibility of future murders should have put a damper on our spirits and our appetites, but not so. Just then, a big-haired, gum-chewing waitress arrived, her arms loaded with a plate of mini barbecue sandwiches, a basket of sweet potato fries and bowls of coleslaw and baked beans. Our table top was lookin' good.

"Compliments of Kenny," she said, nodding toward the bar. "For some reason, he wants to surprise and delight you two." The savory aromas of down home cooking mingled in the warm air and reached our nostrils.

We waved and blew kisses at Kenny, mouthing the word,

"Thanks!"

We dug into the tender and succulent pulled pork. The fries were hot, extra crispy and salty. Murder and wrongful imprisonment be damned! Food was for the hungry.

Chapter 8

Back home alone, I wandered from the living room to the bedroom and back into the living room again. With French gone, I felt anxious, skittish. I was used to being alone—that was the cost of a beautiful life with an important man—but this was horrible. There was a constant chafing at my heart and in my brain. I padded into the kitchen, made myself a cup of tea and took it to the living room.

I sat on the sofa, facing the lake, sipping the hot tea, and tried to calm down. I wondered about French. Would he be in his own cell or in some kind of central holding tank, complete with hardened criminals, drunks and rowdy sailors who abused their town passes from Baldwin Park, the local Naval Training Center?

French was so proper and clean. The worst thing for him would be to stay in a cell with no change of underwear, no shower, no deodorant. And a toothbrush. Did they keep new toothbrushes for the prisoners and hand them out, one by one? If not, this alone could push a man like French over the edge.

French would tire of peanut butter sandwiches, never a favorite with him. Rick had told me this was standard fare in the Orange Avenue hoosegow. No grilled salmon or swordfish from Papa's Place or La Croqueta, our fine dining establishments.

Too bad I couldn't bring him a picnic basket with goodies à la Little Red Riding Hood.

The more I thought about French, the antsier I got. A new thought hit me like a karate chop between my shoulder blades—not Rick, not anybody was going to stop me from going to the jail to see French. I packed a basket of goodies, some fresh underwear and sundries for him, threw my boots back on and ran to my car. As I drove, I thought about French and how he would worry about his hotel. That was French—so dutiful. After that, he might spare a worried thought for me, though he sometimes said I was like a cat—I always landed on my feet.

Right now I was on four wheels, speeding toward my man. Who was on duty at the jail? Seemed like most of the police force was at our hotel. I hoped it might be someone I knew, someone who might cut me some slack.

Chapter 9

My little gambit was a bust, sort of. When I arrived at the jail, I ran into my friend, Brad Yaeger. Brad was the police hypnotist and had helped me overcome my fear of palmetto bugs and other Florida insects. He liked me and he liked French, but he didn't budge. He was in charge of the prisoners and took his assignment seriously.

He told me Rick could have his badge for insubordination if he let me in to see French. I couldn't have that happen, so I backed down. I gave Brad the basket for French.

"Don't you worry, Maya. I'll keep an eye out for him," he said, giving my shoulder a protective pat as he walked me back to my car. "He'll be out in no time. This is all a big mix-up."

I swiped at my eyes and hoped he didn't see. "Okay, Brad. I know I can count on you," and gave him a quick hug before I opened my car door.

Chapter 10

Before I knew it, I was home again, my heart aching even more than it had before. The phone rang and it was Doug Reed. He had been to see French and reported that French was fine. It frustrated me that he had seen French and I had not, but I swallowed the lump in my throat. Hard as it was, I maintained silence.

We hung up and I thought about the receipt and the pantyhose container under my bathroom sink. Hiding those was surely illegal, tampering with evidence or some such thing. But what would have been the point of giving them to Rick? He would have crowed, and I would have been giving him a nail with which to crucify my innocent French. French, who picked up stray spiders in the house with tissues and then tossed them into the shrubbery, rather than kill them.

The phone rang again. This time it was Rick Wells, Orlando PD. He thought it best to keep to the scheduled Manager's Conference events and activities. Tonight the gala dinner dance would happen, as planned.

"I'll be honest with you, Maya," Rick said, "I'm in an odd position here. You're a person of interest but you're also familiar with all the players who will be at this gala."

"Thanks for calling me interesting."

"You know what I mean," he snapped. "Tom and I talked it over and we'd like you to keep your eyes and ears open at the party. You know these people. Try to figure out if any of them are acting out of character and then report back to us what you observed."

"Will do," I said. "I'm happy to help," thinking this was a step in the right direction.

"The wait staff from the banquet department will be peppered with plainclothes officers," he continued, "and the hotel security team will be beefed up with OPD guys."

Rick believed that Torrey's murder was an inside job and I agreed. The killer was probably someone within the upper circles of Sapphire Resorts, someone who would stand to benefit from the death of the president of the company.

Then again, it could have been some woman spurned by Torrey when someone younger and cuter tugged at his babe rader. Torrey had such a short attention span.

The ball would proceed tonight as planned and look like any other hotel gala. It would be in lock down mode but only a few of us would know it.

Chapter 11

In my dressing area, I pulled together my outfit for the dance. Something nagged at me while I laid out my clothes. I called Detective Sergeant Tom Koenig.

"Tom, I'd like to invite two guests to tonight's activities. One is my dear friend, Jake, who works right here on the property as the chief accountant, as you may know. The other is Lily Abbott, the wife of William Abbott, who represents the Norwegian owners. You've met both Lily and Jake on several occasions."

"With all due respect to you, Mrs. French, I'm gonna have to say no. We'll have enough people to watch tonight without two extra heads bobbin' around the room."

"Oh, Tom," I fairly simpered, doing my best Blanche DuBois. My experience with Southern men in authority was that they did not like to be challenged by women. But they were so chivalrous—it was either inborn or fed them in their baby formula—that they would do almost anything for you if you knew how to fake that feminine helplessness with enough sincerity.

"I ask because I need their moral support and help. You and your men will be so busy catching the murderer, that you won't have any time to look in on little old me," I said, feeling just a little cheesy. But hey, I needed his okay.

"You're right about that," he answered, sounding proud. He

was, no doubt, picturing himself in action later tonight, hunting down his prey like a country bloodhound.

I continued, "French won't be there to be my partner and keep me company, so Jake and Lily will take his place, more or less. He'd be pleased to know it takes two people to make up for his absence, wouldn't he?"

"Won't that be one too many people at your table, ma'am?"

"Tom, you know what?" It was important I sound innocent and not contradictory here. It was all in the tone of voice.

I pretended I was Melanie Wilkes from Twelve Oaks and continued, "They'll replace not only French, but Torrey, too. We're going to invent a reason those two scamps have disappeared, aren't we? What story have you made up, by the way?"

"Well, ma'am, I'm right glad you called when you did. You must have that ESP or somethin'. I was just fixin' to call you." He paused for a moment.

"What are we gonna tell 'em?" he continued. I imagined him scratching the back of his head, deep in a perplexing tangle of non-thoughts.

I considered. "Let's say that they've been called away on some sort of official Sapphire Resorts business. Let's borrow another property here in Florida."

"Good," he said.

"Now, what would require they both leave, yet nothing so big that it would have been on the news?" I asked, more of myself than of him.

"You mean like the collapsin' of the atrium bridge that crushed all those poor folks in your Dallas hotel a while back?"

"Right, right. It can't be that big, but something serious— something that might jeopardize the reputation of the hotel— something that Red and French need to handle—" I paused. There was only silence on the other end of the line. I had not expected more.

"I've got it!" I said. "We'll say the Sultan of Barwani was visiting the Coral Gables property, when some jewels belonging to one of his wives went missing from the room safe. Hotel security found the culprit on the engineering staff and returned the jewels. Because the sultan is such a heavy hitter, and he and his entourage mean so much to Sapphire Resorts here and internationally, both Torrey and French were dispatched to smooth things over. They took a chopper from our helipad earlier this evening and are expected back some time later tonight."

"I was just thinkin' somethin' like that myself," Tom said.

Good thing he could not see me rolling my eyes. I still needed his approval before I could invite my friends.

"Tom, what a great idea that was!" I gushed. How did Southern women do this all day? I was nearly dead from the effort. Yet, I continued, "Now, back to my friends... you'll see that they not only keep me company, but also they'll be additional eyes and ears. It's always good to have a likable extra man at a party. Jake's a good dancer; he makes the ladies feel beautiful and that may help him gather some interesting information.

"Lily knows a lot of the Sapphire execs and their spouses already," I added. "She can pump a person for information faster than a sump pump removes sludge from the back of a mobile home." I felt sure he would understand the rustic comparison.

"Well, ma'am. Seein' as how we wouldn't want you to be all alone this evenin', I guess it might be all right," he said.

Whew! *Mission accomplished.* My facial muscles required a splint, after all the phony smiling into the line, but victory was mine.

Chapter 12

My usual worries about my looks and my wardrobe were pre-empted by the number of thoughts and questions swirling in my head. I couldn't get French off my mind. We had to find that killer tonight at the party. We just had to. So many important people were here for the conference, a strangler was on the prowl, and I was all alone and feeling vulnerable. Inside, I was mewling and insecure. Outside, I had ugly, red, itchy splotches all over my midriff; my usual response to stress.

Normally, French and I thought through big problems together. Often, his was the voice of measured logic, whereas my thoughts and feelings collided with one another.

My "aha" moments arrived by special delivery. There was an intuitive alchemy in my brain that threw facts and possibilities together into the hopper. Over time, they came out as a cohesive whole. That didn't mean I wanted to do all the thinking alone. I liked to bounce my abstracts against French's more traditional canvas for a new combo of shapes, colors and forms.

My tea sat next to me, getting cold, as I fiddled with my hair and makeup at the dressing table. First things first. Alana Torrey was due back from Atlanta, where her mom had been in surgery.

Good old Tom from the PD had just called me. He was becoming my new best friend. Pretty amazing, considering he didn't like high teas, line dancing or chick flicks. Or even me, really. Outside of one little murder, we had nothing in common.

He told me something that seemed impossible. "Uh, ya know, Mrs. French, Alana doesn't even know she's a widow yet."

"How could that be?" I couldn't believe it.

"We couldn't find a number for her mom or dad. We don't know what hospital the mom is in."

"That's ridiculous," I said, as undiplomatic as ever.

"It may be," he said, sounding defensive, "but that's the truth. We know her return flight number because your in-house limo was supposed to pick her up from the airport this afternoon."

"I see." I made an effort to be pleasant. "Is there something I can do to help?" I added, as sweet as Florida orange juice.

"As a matter of fact, yes. We're meetin' her at her gate at the airport and givin' her the bad news. Would you come with us? It might be useful, havin' a female there when we tell her."

I got his meaning. He and Rick weren't up to having an hysterical woman on their hands alone. "Sure, Tom," I replied. "I'll be happy to come along."

Alana and I were not close but we had known one another a long time. I guess you could call us corporate acquaintances. She would most likely go into shock, Tom told me.

Unless she's the murderer.

"Really? How could she be the murderer, when she left for Atlanta during the cocktail reception?" A voice piped up in my head.

Then another voice argued, "But she could have arranged the murder, couldn't she? She didn't have to be there personally to make it happen. She just needed an accomplice. What would motivate an accomplice?"

There were so many possibilities—the promise of position,

the promise of power, the promise of prestige, the promise of Alana. My mind darted from Alana and the promises to what would likely happen next.

Alana would probably break down only a little, if at all, at the airport, being the disciplined lady that she was. She would ask to be excused from the evening's festivities. We would have to make a plausible excuse for her. That would be odd. Now there would be three key people missing from the formal affair. Would the other guests buy our stories? Probably. We could easily say Alana had decided to stay on with her mother for another day.

My mind skipped back to French. Why did he have that pesky receipt and the pantyhose box on his desk? Could French have thrown a rod somewhere in that sleek Maserati brain of his? As soon as he got out of jail, would he turn on me like a rabid squirrel? Would he kill me, too? Who really knows another person?

* * *

Rick and Tom need not have worried about Alana making a scene or being hard to comfort. She almost walked past us as she deplaned but I called out to her. She looked surprised to see me and smiled at first. Then, alarm registered on her face. Rick delivered the bad news and she froze for a brief moment, then reached for his right forearm in the most delicate and proper manner. Looking down at his badge and then into his face with her china blue eyes, she blinked hard a few times and in her soft, Georgia peach drawl, said, "Thank you, Chief Wells, for your sensitivity. I feel like I'm in a bad dream." I felt like I might have fainted, had I been given that news about my husband. She was taking this well.

She paused, staring into space, her voice small. "Thank you for bringing Maya along."

With that, she turned to me and slipped her arm under mine. We walked to the baggage carousel in silence, her high heels clicking in a lonely sort of way down the highly polished, linoleum floors.

* * *

Once back on the hotel property, our sad little group pulled up to the private VIP underground entrance of the building. To protect her from prying eyes and to keep her safe, we walked Alana through the back corridors and service elevator to her new, two-story suite, different than the one she had shared with Red.

Rick and Tom did a quick sweep of the rooms before they left us there. Alana said she needed to go upstairs to think and to rest, but would I please stay in the living room downstairs so she didn't feel quite so alone?

I agreed. No need to point out she was not really alone. Plain clothes guards were already in place outside the locked double doors of her suite.

Chapter 13

In Alana's suite, I waited until the crying stopped, then tiptoed upstairs to look in on her. She was resting in the arms of Morpheus, so I left her a note in the kitchen: I've gone home to change for tonight. Rick's men are posted right outside your front doors. You are safe. Call me if you need something. Extension 3101. Love, Maya.

* * *

I had so looked forward to tonight. But now, as I walked through this great hotel in all its architectural magnificence, I felt sad. Sad for Alana. Sad for Redmund, even. Sad that evil had to exist in the world. Sad for French, to be a suspect and to be locked up in a jail cell. I felt a big dose of sad for Maya French, too, but that was called self-pity and there was no time for that. Not now.

I walked through the hotel lobby, stepped onto the down escalator and found myself surrounded by tourists. God bless them. They made our lives possible. Other catty hotel managers and their wives might refer to them as "tourons," but not French and me. We called them manna from heaven.

True, they were often not pretty, especially after a day at the pool. Fried by the sun, with white racing stripes decorating the sides of their arms, torsos and legs where the sun had not hit, they often wandered stiffly around the lobby, looking pink, puffy and pitiful.

Still, they were precious to us. French tried to protect them from themselves. He had initiated the "Sun Squad" at our resort. Attractive young gals and guys, in sun visors, crisp white tennis shorts and matching tank tops, strolled poolside with old-fashioned cigarette trays in front of them. Unlike the hot-chacha girls of the 1940s, these youngsters hawked sunscreen, Bullfrog and aloe vera lotion instead of cigars, cigarettes or Tiparillos.

When the Squad noticed guests snoozing while slowly roasting to a dusky concord grape color, they awakened them and suggested a move to the shade with, perhaps, a soothing refreshment, such as an orange creamsicle smoothie and a foot reflexology massage. Or, how about a strawberry banana rum smoothie and a Balinese body rub under a thatched roof hut, lakeside?

Life hardly got more decadent than this. Our guests deserved it. They worked hard all year, and this was their one treat to themselves and their families. They wanted to be near Disney, but not drowning in all the typical Disney hoopla.

Silver Pines was several cuts above anything Disney had to offer—fun and relaxed, yet elegant and grand. Our job was to make our guests feel as special as they were.

My thoughts of the tourists stopped as my feet touched the bottom of the escalator. I was not far from the OPD's makeshift office, Meeting Room C. Might as well stop by and say hey, see if they'd come up with anything.

Things looked less makeshift than the last time I visited. Detectives were hunkered in front of computers, printers and fax machines that the hotel IT Department had brought down for them. Electrical cords ran this way and that, in front of several desks in the room, creating a wavy, criss-cross pattern that looked like a roller-coaster thrill ride for a little Orlando mouse.

"Mrs. French, so good of you to stop by!" My mouse fantasy was interrupted by Sergeant Tom Koenig. He rose, as best he could, to greet me. "To what do we owe this great honor?" He hiked up his pants by the belt as he spoke.

"Hi there! I thought I'd just drop by to see if you have anything new." Old leather belly was none too pleased to see me. I almost felt sorry for him. Almost. He wanted to be rude. But he was on my turf. My husband was his chief suspect but also, technically, his host. Quite a conundrum. Koenig wanted to make me feel small. I could sense a smugness about him, but Southern manners did not allow biting the hand that feeds you. Indirectly, through French, I was his hostess, too.

Koenig looked uncomfortable. At the same time I entered the room, a well groomed young waiter in formal attire rolled in a large room-service cart, with a white linen tablecloth and one long-stemmed red rose, through the side door of Meeting Room C. He began setting up various sandwiches, a silver punch bowl filled with iced soft drinks and plates of oatmeal raisin and chocolate chip cookies on the banquet table in the back of the room, next to the urns of coffee.

"Here's your Monte Cristo sandwich, Sergeant Koenig!" he said, setting a placemat, a napkin and silverware on Koenig's desk. The waiter returned to the cart, bent at the waist and opened the door of the heating section beneath the tray. He removed a covered plate and, with a flourish, whisked off the silver warming cover. He placed the sandwich with its elaborate garnish and double order of fries on Sergeant Koenig's desk.

"Mmm! That smells good," I said, smiling at Tom.

The Sarge turned, so his mountain of girth was between his plate and me. My timing could not have been better for me or worse for him.

"Enjoy your sandwiches, guys—especially, you, sir!" the waiter said as he wheeled his cart out of the room. "Compliments of Mr. French's staff and Silver Pines."

Nice guy. He nodded and smiled at me before he hurried

out.

Ignoring the waiter, Koenig reached past his plate and took a white sheet of paper from his deck, "We got the goods on the pantyhose. It was manufactured by L'eggs, just as you said. Suntan. Total support."

"Just as I predicted," I answered.

"Not entirely," he drawled at me, with that smugness I had sensed when I entered the room. "They were size B."

"I don't believe it," I said, feigning shocked surprise, though I had already guessed it, after finding the empty pantyhose box on French's desk.

"Yup, that's right. The crime lab in Sanford knows what they're doin'. If they say Size B, then it's Size B. No question."

"Well, I'll be darned," I said, acting impressed.

I wanted to leave now and I wanted to shift the focus from pantyhose to something else. I said my goodbyes and surveyed the banquet table, nabbing an oatmeal cookie on my way out.

"Everything looks *delicious,* guys. Enjoy!" I said as I left, rubbing it in that they were French's guests. Even *in absentia,* he was treating them royally, something that could probably not be said of the way they were treating him back in his cell on Orange Avenue.

Chapter 14

I was rattled by everything that had happened in such a short time. I might not have liked Torrey but he was a human being and someone had offed him in a most peculiar way. Knowing that the murderer was likely going to be at tonight's party, shake my hand or give me a warm embrace and maybe even, if I was wrong and it was a man, take me for a turn or two around the dance floor, was just plain creepy.

Then there was Alana. She would be lying around her suite alone, anguished, hurting. My heart went out to her, yet she was, statistically, the most likely suspect. Earlier, in her suite, hearing her sobs floating down from the bedroom fairly convinced me that she was innocent. But what if murderers had regrets and second thoughts? Couldn't that happen, too? And what if murderers made sure their phony sobs were heard by gullible girls like me? I couldn't help but wonder.

By the time I walked back to the tin-roofed, Grand Floridian cottage that French and I shared on the resort's lake, I was not a happy Sapphire Resorts camper. Rick and Koenig were using me when it was convenient and, otherwise, considered me somewhere between laughable and deplorable. They were more like enemies than allies. If they knew I had a pantyhose box from French's desk under my bathroom sink, they might clamp some cuffs on me and lead me to my own private cell right next to French's 8x8.

Then it hit me. I had to laugh at myself. I was a woman. I wore pantyhose. No one was going to think twice if I had a pantyhose box under my bathroom sink, even if French's fin-gerprints were all over it.

Only I knew it might have the murderer's fingerprints on it, as well. Was there a crash course in fingerprint identity that I could take? Or had I already smudged them beyond recogni-tion? What a bad mistake I had made, if that were true. Maybe I *did* deserve to go to jail. I told myself it didn't really matter. The murderer would probably do or say something tonight to give her or himself away.

Ten minutes of meditative sleep would lift me out of my slump. I needed to be sharp tonight. As I drifted off counting backwards from ten to one, I cheered myself with the thought of Jake and Lily flanking me at tonight's gala.

Jake and I met in an eighth grade English class. Throughout high school, we were like Siamese twins, joined at our twisted brains. Physical opposites, he was tall and fair-haired, with broad shoulders and long legs. He was a cliché—unavailable to girls—and t'was such a pity.

Lily and I met at Silver Pines during the pre-opening of the resort. Both executive wives with a renegade streak, we enjoyed similar lives and had the same irreverence for things hotel and corporate. Soon, we were as close as the eyes of a halibut.

Jake, Lily and I shared a black humor and, together, we had more fun than was allowed. Tonight, the mood might be more serious. If we were on our game, we might solve a murder.

I awoke a short while later, feeling refreshed. I made myself a cup of tea and, for what seemed like the tenth time in a twenty-four hour period, I freshened up, put on my face and coiffed my 'do.'

Now for the gown. Layers of royal blue chiffon cascaded from my shoulders into a deep V just above my waist, tightly cinched by an obi sash of the same fabric. The chiffon continued in a long, loose skirt that swirled at my ankles, showing off my dyed-to-match, *peau de soie* heels. The color accented my thick, auburn hair, and the proportions of the ensemble accented my small, but shapely, shape.

Diamond drop earrings and an oval, rhinestone-studded Judith Leiber bag completed the ensemble. For once, appraising myself in the full-length mirror, I didn't feel too short, too fat, too plain or too anything. *It figures. I've never looked this good, might never look this good again, and French isn't here to see me.*

* * *

Knots of beautiful people in floor-length gowns and black tuxedos stood chatting in the ballroom, still holding their champagne glasses from the pre-gala reception.

Each weighty ceiling chandelier was polished to glittering perfection. The house lights were low, and the table top decor of softly draped metallic satins picked up the golden light of tea candles in crystal holders. The white rose and orchid centerpieces were positioned to reflect their richness on gold-trimmed mirrors. The china, flatware and wine glasses offered an invitation to an elegant evening. Jake rose as I approached our table for ten. Lily and he had left a seat open between them.

Any one of the seven little dwarves who would be seated at our table could be a killer. As I waited for people to arrive, my heart beat in a hurried, uneven rhythm. It wasn't every night you purposefully set out to trip up a murderer.

There would be plenty to drink, a new wine with every course of the meal, then cordials and brandy with dessert. I wasn't a big drinker at any time, but tonight I would go through the motions, putting various glasses to my lips but not taking one sip. I wanted all of my senses to be acute and engaged.

Had French been next to me where he belonged, we would be seated near the Torreys, but not necessarily at the same table. They were usually surrounded by local politicians and high society. The Torreys also imported a cadre of senators, philanthropists and middling to major celebrities wherever they went. They were in the outer social register ionosphere and we orbited nearby.

Tonight, our table included upper level Sapphire Hotels execs and some local bigwigs, with whom we were friendly. Here came Giorgio and Iris Pappas, an older couple from Orlando. She was all gussied up in her sequined gown, her Olympia blue eye shadow, her heavily penciled brows and her hairpiece, that she had probably been wearing since her go-go days in the 60s. Giorgio was wiry and happy. Iris was plump and happy. They were both disappointed to hear that French had been unavoidably detained in Coral Gables.

Then the Messinas arrived, Frankie and Linda. Frankie had worked for Sapphire forever. My skin felt prickly whenever Frankie got near me, but Linda was like cool water, Eurasian, an exotic Ingrid Bergman. Her shiny black hair was pulled back into a thick, glamorous knot at the nape of her neck, which was festooned with large, perfectly matched, cultured pearls. I wanted to *be* Linda when I grew up. Except, what was she doing with Frankie? I always wondered about that.

Frankie was slick bordering on smarmy. Immaculately attired at all times, he knew everyone and had only wonderful things to say. Still, anyone could tell that he would chop off and sell Linda's beautiful black braid for a penny, if he thought it might get him one eyelash closer to Redmund Torrey. Then, there were the whisperings that he came from a big Sicilian family, and we all knew what that meant...

I watched him with alert eyes, as he seated Linda and then stretched out his heavily bejeweled left hand to me, giving my right hand the old backwards sissy shake, which I have always hated.

"Maya, you look absolutely radiant tonight!" he cooed, giving me an appreciative yet very proper smile, as he straightened the cuffs of his shirt. Tainted at his core, Frankie was all about looking good on the outside. "Where's French?" His hands went to his bow tie, checking to see if it were straight.

"Called away on business," I answered, going into my little spiel for the night, while I hid my upset behind a trouper's resigned smile.

The Luzis, Vacaar and Mona, were also guests at our table. They were Sapphire Resorts people, stationed in the Midwest. Vacaar was a Regional VP with his eyes set on bigger sights. He was a sharp guy, who had come up from nothing in an Albanian village on the Adriatic.

He rushed over, leaving Mona chatting with someone else, and greeted me formally with a slight accent, "You look beautiful tonight, Miss Maya. Where is that husband of yours?"

"Oh gosh, he's on special assignment with Torrey in Coral Gables. I guess it's just us chickens tonight." I was almost ready for my Oscar.

"If you need me to step in to make announcements, speeches, anything at all, you give me a nod."

His wife walked over. He said with a grin, "Why, look, Miss Maya. Here comes my beautiful daughter, Mona. Say hello to her, would you?"

Mona flashed that megawatt smile and her long, tanned legs peeked out from the slit on the side of her sequined, ruby, sheath. How a compact guy like Vacaar ever scored a retired, super model wife like Mona was a mystery to everyone. He never took his eyes off her. Maybe that was part of his charm for her. As I air kissed Mona, I stole a sidelong glance at Vacaar. What would a man like Luzi stand to gain by Torrey's death? Was there anything in it for Mona?

Chapter 15

"Look who's here!" Jake and Lily whispered into my ears at the same instant, causing me to bounce up from my truffled risotto appetizer. There stood Alana Torrey, framed in the grand entry doors to the ballroom and bathed in soft chandelier light. Shimmering like liquid gold as she approached, she glided, she floated. No other woman moved with her poise.

She was a goddess in motion. Her gown was a slender silhouette, champagne colored, dripping with bugle beads that swayed ever so gently with each step. Her bag matched her shoes and gown. Her clear complexion was complimented by her crown of thick, shoulder-length, rich girl hair. She was regal and that was the reason she reigned as the queen of Sapphire Hotels and Resorts. The only things missing were her scepter and crown.

"Oh my gosh!" slipped from my lips, as I looked at her in wonderment.

Lily asked in a whisper, "Bollocks, has she come downstairs to join us at this party, no matter what? 'The show must go on' and all that rot?"

"Stunning!" came from Jake's mouth. His gaze was almost envious.

She either has the discipline of ten Olympian athletes or

*she's not distraught because she knows who murdered Red—
she did!*

As she approached the table next to ours, I rose and intercepted her.

"Alana! I never expected to see you here tonight," I said, giving her an air kiss and a little hug.

Her whisper in my ear was soft but clear. "I want everything to appear normal. Just because Redmund isn't here doesn't mean I can neglect our guests. Besides, I want to find that murderer as much as anyone else—more than anyone else. Maybe someone won't be able to look me in the eye tonight. It wouldn't help Redmund for me to stay up in our suite, crying like a whiney baby."

I smiled at her and said, "Got it." She and I understood each other. She was a steel magnolia and I stood in awe of her.

Sitting at a nearby table were the Trotters, Philip and Chloe. Philip was second in command to Torrey and, as such, Torrey's right hand man. He was Executive Vice-President and he oversaw the entire Sapphire Hotels and Resorts nation, all ninety-two properties.

"Alana, come sit next to Chloe and me right here," I overheard him say as he stood up to greet her, ever the British gent. As always, he was solicitous of Alana. *Certainly more so tonight,* I observed, *since she's alone.*

He's so ambitious. He and his sparkling wife, Chloe, were both as polished as ivory chess pieces. Philip relied on his British accent and his Southern belle wife to push them both forward in life. The two of them stood to gain a lot with Torrey gone.

After the entrée, it was time to dance. Jake excused himself to pick a beauty out of the crowd, while Lily and I chatted about this and that, all the while observing those around us, as though we worked for the CIA. Many of the servers and security people passing through the room were Rick's deputies. While serving soufflés, they were also taking mental notes, I supposed.

"May I have this dance?" a deep, rich baritone enveloped me. I looked up into the warm brown eyes of Brett Fitzpatrick, one of my favorite men of Sapphire Resorts. His wife, Diane, could be a bit of a pill. Maybe I would be, too, if my husband had shoulders so wide he had to go through doors at an angle and women threw themselves at him. And he were constantly catching them, midair.

"Of course, my friend!" I answered, thrilled to jump to my feet, not only for a needed stretch, but also for the chance to look at all those potential murderers from a different angle.

"Maya, you are beautiful and as light as a cream puff in my arms and probably twice as yummy," Brett said to me, smiling with both his lips and his chocolatey eyes.

"Brett," I said. "You are a shameless flatterer, and really corny but, hey—don't stop!" We both laughed.

French had told me long ago that Fitz was like a big, snuggly teddy bear. Women loved to hold him close and he loved to be held.

What does Brett have that makes a gal want to melt into him? What makes him cuddly, while Torrey's vibe was always lecherous and icky?

Brett kept me swirling and dipping, my gown floating gracefully along behind me, until I felt like a professional ballroom dancer. At a slow point in one of our sweeping turns, I cast a glance at a nearby table. There sat Brett's wife, Diane, giving me the old stink eye.

Didn't she know that I love my French? That I have no designs on her old teddy bear of a husband? Not every woman is trying to get into his tighty whites. I tried to beam my thoughts to her as I waved and smiled.

She sat there with a dark cloud wrapped around her bitter little shoulders. *I haven't walked in her shoes,* I reminded myself. *I don't know what it feels like to suspect that every attractive woman I see might have recently enjoyed my husband's charms.* And I liked it that way. That was part of what was so lovable about French. He was true blue. He was mine. There wouldn't be anybody fluffing his covers but me. No need to stare, glare or share when it came to French.

Brett interrupted my thoughts. "So what do you think of those two slackers, Torrey and French, sneaking off to Coral Gables like that and leaving us here all alone to fend for ourselves?"

I shrugged my shoulders, as if to say, "Who knows? Who cares?" Maybe Fitz would say something revealing.

"Well I, for one, miss them both *terribly*, even if you don't." he said, laughing at his own joke. With them gone, he was the alpha male at this event, free to pick and choose female company as he saw fit.

Could a man like this kill his boss? He seemed too relaxed to care enough about prestige, power or personal issues to ever want to pull off a murder. My take on Fitz was that he was a very happy man. But Diane, now that was another matter altogether. She had been beautiful once, but now, like a good wine gone bad, she was sour, after a few too many years with Mr. Wonderful.

Chapter 16

The dance broke up well before midnight, no thanks to *me* or *my* friends. We could have gone on. No one even offered to have an after-party party in a suite, something that used to happen with regularity, like teen acne on Friday evenings before a date.

I left the party scratching my head. Who was the murderer? She or he *had* to be among us. There was no other answer, was there?

Lily and Jake said they would come by my house for a few minutes after the room cleared out. Right now, Jake was flirting with someone. With the house lights up, Lily was checking out all the gowns and shoes, as the last of the guests filed past her to their rooms.

As I left the dance, I passed Rick Wells in the ballroom lobby talking with some partygoers. We made eye contact and gave each other an almost imperceptible shrug that said, "Nothing solid on the radar. Talk to you soon."

I walked toward the porte cochère and the path that led to my home, wondering where I had messed up. Why had I come up empty with no idea about who the murderer was? How much longer would French have to sit in jail? I felt agitated and depressed at the same time, my mind cluttered with opposing thoughts and my heart heavy. I felt a headache starting at the base of my skull.

As I walked the path to my home, one of Rick's men followed me in a golf cart. Just as I arrived at our garden gate, click! It unlocked. He must have buzzed me in via remote control. I gave a little half-wave of thanks without turning around.

* * *

The kettle was starting to boil and I had already changed into something casual when I heard a commotion outside. Racing around the corner from the kitchen to the entry, I saw six people silhouetted near the lamp posts of our entry gate. One of them was wearing a long gown.

I opened the double doors onto the still-moist Central Florida night. "Hey, hey—what's going on?" I asked, as I half-jogged toward the group.

"Mrs. French, we caught these interlopers trying to force their way onto your property, ma'am." a man in a hotel uniform answered.

"Bill, is that you?" I asked. I recognized him as one of Rick's men and I heard Jake's and Lily's excited voices.

"We tried to explain that we're your friends." Jake's voice rose above Lily's.

"They didn't believe us, Maya. They drew their damned guns, the bloody cretins. Do they think we're in the Wild West here?" Lily huffed, indignant.

"Okay, okay. No harm done. It's just a little misunderstanding!" I tried to calm everyone.

"Guys, these two are my friends and I invited them over for a nightcap. I'm okay. They're okay. You can put your guns away," I told the four "groundskeepers." The kerfuffle was over.

"Thank you, thank you. Thank you for protecting me!" I said sincerely to the PD guys in disguise.

PD guys in disguise, I thought as Jake and Lily followed me into the house and the undercover men disappeared into the bushes. *That Rick! Imagine making these guys in grounds-keeper uniforms hide near the water's edge at night, when our little lake is Water Moccasin Heaven. What the heck is he thinking? And what are they thinking? Not about their own safety, that's for sure. I hope I conveyed my gratitude properly to those men.*

Jake, Lily and I sat around the great room coffee table in overstuffed chairs and sipped our fresh brewed tea, spiked with a generous shot of Myers's Rum. They were filling me in on what they had seen at the party. They talked over each other like kindergarteners at show and tell, vying for my attention. In the end, there was silence. We stared at the walls and furnishings.

"So, it boils down to this—" I looked at both of them in turn, "neither one of you got the goods on anyone, right?"

"Yeah, that's right," they both mumbled, looking down, disappointed.

"Don't look so glum, chums," I said. "I didn't figure anything out, either. Whoever the murderer is, she or he is one cool customer."

"There was one odd thing," Lily said, sitting up straight. "I just remembered! That little Dapper Dan, oh what is his name? The one with the retired supermodel wife from Denmark..."

"Vacaar Luzi?" I said, hopefully.

"Yes, that's the one! He danced with me and right toward the end of the dance, he leaned into me and held me a little closer. I thought he was going to get fresh but he said, 'I have something I need to tell Maya. Ask her to meet me tomorrow in our suite after my round of golf and lunch, around three.'

"I asked him if he wouldn't rather talk to you now but he said no, this was not the time nor place. It could wait."

"No kidding? He must know something. After golf and lunch, huh? Golf and lunch always come first with these guys. The earth could be on a collision course with Asteroid Giganticus but nothing would interfere with their game and their yapping about it afterward over lunch."

We settled back into silence, sipping and thinking. The evening was a dud. We were no smarter now than we were five hours earlier. At least we were well-fed and well-danced. Maybe Luzi would crack the case wide open. Maybe he knew who the killer was. Maybe, maybe, maybe. After a while, Jake and Lily said good-night and left.

I slipped into my nightgown and between my Egyptian cotton hotel sheets. I turned toward French's side of the bed.

"French, honey," I said. "I'm so sorry. We didn't get much tonight. Maybe Vacaar will provide the missing puzzle piece. For now, it's just worry and wait." The tears came then but I brushed them away. *No! No tears. Just action. Tomorrow we get this bastard or bastardess.* "I promise!" I said it out loud.

French was having none of it. No answer. Just his empty side of the bed, his pillow untouched. I closed my eyes but sleep did not come. It was hard to wait but at least I didn't have to wait long.

Chapter 17

It was early on Sunday morning when I called Reed at home.

"Reed. How are you? I didn't wake you, did I?" I asked.

"No," he said, asleep. "I was awake."

"Just reading the Bible, huh?" I asked.

"That's right," he said. "Why are you calling me at home, this early and on a Sunday yet?"

"Why do you think? I miss my husband."

"Oh, yeah, him," he said and yawned.

"I haven't heard from you since Friday evening. What exactly are you doing for French?"

"I am doing everything I can, Maya. Trust me."

"You sound relaxed," I said, with attitude. "Too relaxed. Aren't you the one who told me that 'Trust me' is legalese for 'Screw you'?"

No response.

"Hello, Doug. Maya to Doug," I called to him, "Are you still on the line?" I should be nicer to the man who was fighting for French's freedom.

"Give me a break, Maya. It's too early in the morning for a duel. I'm going to get French out of that sinkhole before you know it. There have been a few twists and turns but it's all okay now."

"What twists and turns?"

"Nothing, really. Nothing worth mentioning. I'm sorry I did."

"Oh, great. Don't go all 'oh so mysterioso' on me, Reed. You're better than that," I said, feeling an urge to reach through the phone and shake him.

"Look, Maya, it's just boring legal stuff. I took care of it."

"Okay," I sighed.

"I'll call you as soon as French is released," he assured me, then added, "You still like shoes, don't you, Maya?"

"Yes, Doug. I still like shoes." He was getting tedious.

"He'll be waiting for you to pick him up on Orange Avenue before you can go to Dillard's to buy a new pair of shoes."

Then he added, "Trust me," and laughed.

We said our goodbyes and hung up. I wondered if Dilly's had any pointy toed boots suitable for kicking attorneys in their briefs?

* * *

There was an event later this morning for the Sapphire Hotels and Resorts female managers and executive wives at the hotel. Someone in charge of such things had decided it would be nice to get in a color expert to analyze the ladies' colors.

I knew this "color expert" from my California days. She was friendly with the Torreys. Darla was an older blonde babe with squinty little eyes. She had reinvented herself a few times since I met her. At first, her beau had been an older goodfella who lived in La Costa and she called herself his assistant. A few years later, she traded him in for a different wise guy who owned a fashionable eatery in Rancho Mirage and she was the hostess. Her latest boyfriend owned hair salons and now she was a "color expert." I couldn't believe they flew her in from California for this. She was a schemer, all right. Her men were always married, just not to her. She lived around the fringes and put on airs. We were not each other's biggest fans.

It was part of my job description as First Lady of Silver Pines to attend all such corporate events, no matter what else might be happening in my life. The good news was, I would get a look at all the hotel wives and the female managers in a relaxed group setting. After the colors, I had invited them to join me at Papa's Place, a themed restaurant perched on the cliffs, overlooking the resort's lake.

We had been given strict instructions—bare, naked faces. Makeup artists would be applying our new colors with a trowel, once Darla determined whether we were spring, summer, autumn or winter. For the occasion, I decided on a white gauze ensemble and sling-back Italian sandals. I wore my long hair off my shoulders and looked cool and casual, like I stepped straight out of a Ronrico Rum ad.

* * *

"Everyone, come gather 'round," Darla called to the ninety or so ladies in her oversized penthouse suite turned color salon. "I want you all to see something."

I sat on a salon chair with swatches of different colored fabrics draped over my shoulders and across my neck. Darla had me by the chin whiskers.

"Have a look at Maya here," she addressed the group in a loud voice. "Maya is an 'autumn.' This explains why she always looks so *sallow*. I've always wondered why Maya looks so *sallow*. Well, this is why!"

A gasp went around the room.

She went on, "An autumn can never wear *these* colors." She then rotated all the jewel toned fabrics past my neck and face.

"Further, an autumn can never wear these *cool* tones because cool tones wash out an autumn completely." A look of pity played across her face, as she held the cool tones against my cheek.

"Then, to further complicate things for poor Maya, look at this!" She gleamed a wicked smile. "Even though Maya has the standard *sallow* autumn coloring on her neck, arms and parts of her face, she also has a ruddy hue on her cheeks that can make her look rough, raw and even rather coarse," she said, puckering her lips in distaste.

I heard soft murmurings around me.

"Ladies, one more thing," she crowed, "don't be like poor Maya and wear white, if your teeth have a yellowish cast to them. Never *ever* wear a shade of white that is brighter than your own teeth."

With that, she turned to me and smiled her very white smile.

"Thank you for volunteering, Maya. My girls can help you select the earth tones that flatter an autumn complexion with ruddy highlights. Next!"

I thanked her and slipped out of the demo chair.

Pretending to be even-complected, I stood tall and cut through the crowd. Obediently, I headed for Darla's assistants, who would probably place a burlap sack over my head to cover the yellow-toothed, *sallow*, nightmare that was me.

Someone in the crowd followed me and grabbed my hand.

"I wonder how you ever dare to leave the house, you poor *sallow* thang," Alana drawled, a little twinkle in her sad and puffy eyes.

"Ya got me," I answered. "I guess I'm just naturally shameless on top of being naturally sallow—and ruddy." We grinned at each other.

"Don't mind her," Alana continued. "She's a nasty old bitch."

"Hey, I thought you got her this gig. Isn't Darla your friend?" I asked.

"Sure she is. But she's still a nasty old bitch." Alana winked, turned and walked away.

Chapter 18

Dave Enderly, French's second-in-command, called me at home.

"Hi, Dave," I said. "You're one lucky guy to reach me. I just stopped in for a moment between having my colors done and hosting a ladies' luncheon at Papa's Place."

"Luck had nothing to do with it, Maya." Dave's baritone boomed into the phone. "Rick has some of his guys tailing you everywhere you go on property. And I have some of my guys tailing Rick's guys."

I laughed. "So, everywhere I go, I trail a long line of 'gardeners' and other hotel staff?"

"That's right!" he said. "You ought to look behind you sometime. It's like you're the Pied Piper of Silver Pines."

That was a funny image, all those guys trailing after me. I laughed and wondered if I should lead them on a merry chase the next time I went somewhere. I could bob and weave through these grounds like a palmetto bug on speed. I knew this place like I knew the new fall collection of St. John's Knits.

I turned my attention to Dave. "I want to compliment you on how you're running things in French's absence. He's going to be so proud of you when he gets back."

"Oh, Maya. Do you really think so? I want to do everything

right. I don't want to screw anything up. He's the one who trained me so I hope I'm doing well. Plus," he added, almost apologetically, "this meeting is a chance to make a name for myself. It could help my career big-time."

"You are, you are, Dave. You're doing everything right. The place is spinning smooth like a gyroscope. The higher ups will notice you, for sure." Dave was a little insecure but that was part of his aw, shucks charm. Underneath his insecurity was a man driven to achieve.

Dave had come to us from our Vermont property, Sapphire Stowe Mountain, where he had learned how to run a four-season resort and, so important to a great career in the industry, how to properly kowtow to monied and spoiled guests.

He and his wife, Margie, were a nice couple with two young children. We sometimes had dinner together at their cottage near the lake in Windermere, or they would come to our place for barbecue during low season.

Once in a while, when her kids were at school, Margie and I floated around Lake Butler for a few hours in her pontoon boat with sandwiches and iced tea.

"I saw the spread you put out for the Orlando PD in Meeting Room C yesterday afternoon, Dave. Great job. You're taking good care of them," I said.

"Thanks, Maya. It means a lot coming from you. I have to take good care of them, don't I? They're going to let French out of jail and they're going to get the murderer."

"They sure are. I also want to compliment you on the dinner dance last night. It was elegant. Everything ran like a Swiss monorail. No one would guess French was not behind it all. You and your team are tight."

"I'm trying, Maya. But, you know, that's why I'm calling you. I'm getting as nervous as a hooker in church. It's nerve-wracking. When are they going to let French out? Do you have any idea?"

"No, Dave, I don't. It *is* nerve-wracking. I feel the same way.

Doug Reed, our attorney, is working on French's release. I don't know what the problem is. I called Reed this morning and he said he's on it."

"Does he think French'll get sprung soon?" Dave asked.

"That's what he keeps telling me," I said.

Dave was so anxious to do right, it could backfire. The resort could not afford for him to lose his cool. He was the guy in charge. He had to keep himself together.

"Listen, Dave," I said, trying to both encourage and reassure him, "you're doing a top flight job. The best way for you to honor French is to take some deep breaths and keep on keepin' on. You're a pro. You can handle this. He'll be back before you can shake a green tambourine."

"I hope so. It gives me the willies to think that one of these Sapphire people could be a murderer. I look at every single one of them and think, *Is it you? Is it you? Is it you?* I feel like my head's about to split open."

Wow, he was in worse shape than I would have expected. He was raising my own anxiety level. I was running out of cheer and this call was taking longer than I wanted. "Dave," I said, "French will be let out of jail tomorrow. I feel it in my bones."

"Oh, thank God." His voice sounded more relaxed already. "It's driving me nuts. I haven't been home since Friday night. The kids miss me. I miss them. Margie could tell something was up at the ball last night. I feel like a criminal for not telling her anything. It's a mess. Boy, will I be happy to see French."

"You and me both, Dave. You and me both."

"Oh, I almost forgot," Dave said. "Vacaar Luzi asked me to come up to his suite around 3:00 p.m. this afternoon. He said you might be there, too. Do you think he has a complaint about the property?"

"No, I don't know what he wants. I'll see you there. I've got to run now before I'm late to my own luncheon. Bye." I hung up.

Why would Vacaar Luzi invite David Enderly and me to his

suite? Would Mona be there, too? I'd see her at Papa's in a few minutes but we wouldn't get a chance to talk privately.

I didn't have time to think about that right now. I had to dive into my closet and find an ivory-colored ensemble or something in earth-tones so I could disguise my tragic sallow-ruddiness. Oh, and I had to see my dentist. These nasty old plywood teeth had to go.

Chapter 19

I looked after my guests, then sat at my table. Papa's had reserved two-thirds of the restaurant for us. We had privacy and, at the same time, all the floor-to-ceiling doors were open to the lake and the pool below and the sweet afternoon breeze. Ultrafine mesh screens kept out the flying insects and the whole shack, perched on the rocks with its tin roof and slow-moving ceiling fans, felt like a little piece of Papa Hemingway's Key West.

On any other day, I was all about the outstanding seafood at Papa's. This was the first time I didn't give a flying Frisbee for what I ate. I was watching people like a cat watches a moth fluttering against a window pane. I was studying their mannerisms, how they spoke to one another, how they shifted their eyes and held their bodies.

I had invited Lily once again. Technically, she was not a Sapphire lady, but who was going to challenge me? I was French's wife and he was the boss of this property. I seated her on the opposite side of the room. She knew what she was supposed to do.

On one level, the luncheon went well. Usually, Sapphire women moved food around their plates in a casual fashion for twenty minutes, while chatting. Today, the ladies all ate with a gusto that was rarely seen in our competitive, skinny-bitch-not-eating-a-thing world.

During the dessert course, four to six Sapphire women commonly shared one of the richest desserts on the menu. Each tried one bite and moaned in appreciation. Then, they set their forks down in unison and smiled at each other, knowing they were the queens of self-discipline. Not today. This day, they could have been training for the Great Salmon Feed and Key Lime Pie Olympics.

On a personal level, the luncheon was a bust. Once again, I felt the heaviness of disappointment settle on my shoulders. Could they all be innocent? I felt so sure a woman had killed Torrey. I thought I understood human behavior. No one seemed off or nervous or suspicious. I felt let down and deflated, once again.

As lunch was wrapping up, I ran into Lily in the powder room of Papa's. "What say we steal away in a few moments and you come with me to the Torreys' original suite? Orlando PD has had it locked and sealed since Red's death." I whispered, making sure no one in the stalls overheard us.

"How are we going to get in?" Lily asked, looking a little hesitant.

"I have my ways, silly, come on. It'll be fun. I have some time before I meet Dave Enderly at Luzi's suite. Remember? They just happen to be on the same floor."

"Oh, all right. Why do I let you talk me into these things?" she said to her own reflection in the mirror, giving her lips a fresh coat of ginger peach gloss.

"Because they're *exciting*." I chided her as I left. "Meet me in the lobby in ten minutes."

* * *

Once Lily arrived, we sauntered through the door to the left of the front desk. If anyone had asked, we would have said we were looking for Jake. We were in luck—no one asked and we managed to give the guys tailing me the slip.

We turned past the marketing and PR offices and then took the service elevator to seventeen. We walked down the hall on little cat feet toward what had been Torrey's original suite.

In my summer tote, I had my handy-dandy skeleton key and a few other little devices. The best one was my bump key. The Orlando PD had installed a dead bolt lock on the service entry door of the suite. This might deter the average burglar, but not me.

Lily watched in wonder as I placed the bump key into the dead bolt and tapped it with a rubber hammer. The service door opened into the kitchen of the suite, as I gave it a little push.

"I say, old bean," she said, "that's pretty impressive. How'd you know it would work?"

"I didn't, but it's not the only tool in my kit, you know." I gave her a nudge that said, "What? You doubted me?"

We stepped into the middle of the kitchen and looked around.

"Kind of feels like Christmastide, don't it?" said Lily.

"Yup, it does," I agreed.

Every surface in the kitchen was covered with a thick layer of white. There were marks and mars where OPD had dusted for prints. The black granite countertops, the stovetop, the stainless steel sinks, the cherry wood cabinet doors were all streaked with white, as was the black refrigerator. The snow-covered vista looked as if it had been smudged by a young Helen Keller, feeling for something to eat.

"Here," I said to Lily, handing her two latex gloves. "Put these on over that perfect manicure of yours." She did, as did I.

"Let's go upstairs to see the bedroom, the closet and the bathroom," I said.

I led and she followed. The bedsheets were crumpled. With my gloved fingers, I smoothed them and noticed a stain. No surprise there. I already suspected that Torrey had enjoyed his murderer just before she killed him. Still, it was gross. Why hadn't the police taken that sheet into evidence? Sloppy police work or was something else at play here?

Lily made a sucking sound as she inhaled and said, "The randy bugger—how disgusting."

"So it is, my dear. Thank God they didn't let Alana back in here," I said, and re-crumpled the sheets.

We opened the closet doors and looked inside. There was nothing out of the ordinary—some well-tailored men's suits, some golf shirts, khakis and casual wear. Torrey's shoes were neatly lined up, all in a row.

Secretly checking out a dead man's wardrobe was a little uncomfortable, like wearing a pair of ballerina flats a half size too small. We both felt it.

"What are we looking for, exactly?" Lily asked.

I looked down at Torrey's foppish velvet slippers with their glittering crests and pointed them out to Lily. "Prince Horny won't be needing these anymore," I said.

Lily giggled. "Seriously, Miss Maya Marple," she said, "why did you bring me here?"

"I'm not sure. It just seemed like we should take a peek."

I walked into the bathroom and began opening drawers.

"Help me look in these," I said to Lily.

"What's this?" she asked, after rummaging through the drawer closest to the spa tub. She held up what looked to be a tiny metal shovel or scraper with a miniature razor blade in it.

"I have no idea," I answered. "Let's commit it to memory and scat. I have to meet Vacaar and David in a few minutes. You go back to the lobby."

Lily smiled at me. "I'm dismissed, am I? No problem—I'm ready to go, thank you!"

Chapter 20

On the way to my appointment, I looked into my tote bag. The silk scarf was neatly in place, covering my burglar's tools and the two sets of latex gloves. No one was going to guess that I had been snooping around Torrey's old suite.

I thought about Vacaar. Why would he tell Lily to tell me to meet him? Why didn't he tell me himself? Maybe the opportunity had not presented itself at the dance. After all, Mona took most of his time and attention and I had been busy observing as many of our Sapphire guests as possible.

And why, of all people, had Vacaar asked David Enderly to meet us in his suite? He couldn't have known that Dave was in charge of everything since French was off the premises, could he? Maybe Vacaar didn't want to meet me in his suite alone. That made sense. Then again, he could have had Mona there as a sort of neutral third party. Did he have something to tell us he would rather not discuss in front of her? My mind was working overtime.

French called my brain the "Big Deal Manufacturing Plant" and, further, said it was a dangerous neighborhood; I should not go there alone. Could I help it that all my synapses and dendrites were well-oiled and ready to pounce on interesting bits of stimulus?

"Oh pshaw! Maybe my manufacturing plant will observe and process something that saves the day," I told French mentally, as I walked down the hall.

I turned the corner which lead to Vacaar and Mona's seventeenth floor suite with its unobstructed view of our property, the pine forest beyond it and Epcot's silver geodesic dome, sparkling in the sun, beyond that. David Enderly stood outside the door, almost vibrating.

Enderly. Why is he such a train wreck? What, really, does he have to be nervous about? Vacaar wields no power over him. Even if Vacaar were to criticize the hotel or last night's event in French's absence, what difference would it make?

"Hi, Maya!" Enderly said, his face relieved to see me.

"Why so nervous, Dave?"

He answered in a hurried stage whisper, his words tumbling out. "Gosh, Maya, wouldn't you be nervous, too? There's a murderer on the loose somewhere. My boss is gone and for the first time ever, I'm in charge of this whole enchilada. If that weren't bad enough, all the big shots from the corporate office and the Weinsteins are here, not to mention the Norwegian owners. I'm on the hot seat. I want to look my best for everyone." He adjusted his tie and gave me a look that said, "You may be the boss's wife but you're a bit dim."

"Okay, I get it," I said. "Take a deep breath and exhale slowly. Let's knock on this door and see what Luzi wants."

He knocked. We stood there and waited. He knocked again. We waited some more.

"Dave, I don't think he's in his suite. Should we just come back in a few minutes?" I suggested.

"Let me call him on the house phone." Enderly said, trotting down the hall toward the elevators. I saw him dial and wait for several rings. He came back, walking slowly.

"This is odd," he said. "There's no answer and Mr. Vacaar was so insistent that I be here at 3:00 p.m. He even left me a voice mail while having lunch at the club house. That was at

1:00 p.m. I'm sure he must be back by now."

"Well then, I authorize you to put your staff key into the door and open it. Pop your head into the entry and call his name," I said.

David followed my direction and waved me in behind him when there was no answer.

"You call out to him, Maya. Go ahead. I think I hear a TV upstairs in the bedroom. Maybe he's in the shower."

"Vaca-a-a-r," I called. No answer. "Mona-a-a." No answer.

"Anybody home?" I shouted, a little louder.

Dave and I looked at each other. I took a few steps into the living room and he followed me. All was in apple pie order. The rooms had been cleaned and the amenities refreshed. A Murano glass platter of sliced exotic fruits sat on the dining room table with a note from the food and beverage department. A bottle of Dom was chilling in a silver ice bucket. The ice was fresh. Room service had been here only a short while ago.

"Go upstairs, Dave. See what's up," I instructed. "Why is that TV on, anyway?"

He did as I asked, then called to me to come up.

"Is it creepy?" I asked before I was halfway up the stairs.

"No. There's nothing creepy," he said.

I walked into the neat bedroom. Housekeeping had made the bed and plumped the pillows. I walked past the closet and into the bathroom.

"*This* is a little creepy." David said. "Look around. The TV is on a golf tournament. The shower door is open. The inside of the shower is wet. The bath mat has footprints on it. There's a wet towel on the floor in front of the sink." He pointed things out as he named them. "Someone showered here just now, most likely Mr. Luzi. You can still feel the humidity in the air—"

"But no one is here." I finished his thought. "Where is he?"

I had the urge to call Luzi like I might call a cat, "Here, Luzi, Luzi, Luzi—" but I didn't.

Instead, I reached into my tote and pulled out my latex

gloves. David had exited the bathroom and walked out onto the oversized deck, perhaps thinking that Luzi was there, taking some air.

I slid on the gloves and opened the bi-fold doors of the closet in the dressing area. All seemed to be in order. But wait—not quite. There was a foot in a high-heeled, sling-back pump sticking out below the hanging clothes. I stared at the foot. I stared at the shoe, buttercup yellow, calfskin, in pristine condition. I pushed the hangers aside to get a better look. I had to know whose foot it was.

Luzi's! Ugh. Ugh. Eeew. There he lay, a vision in yellow, with a fetching plastic bag over his head. I let out a scream that no one heard.

I ran into the bedroom, panic crawling over my skin like a thousand tiny spiders, and yelled for David. Over and over, I yelled but he heard nothing, as he had closed the sliding glass doors behind him.

"Dave, Dave, get in here," I yelled, as I pushed the heavy doors open and ran onto the patio.

He turned, saw me crying and came running to help. "Maya, what is it?" he asked, his voice rising in panic with mine.

"Vacaar's in the closet, dead," I gasped. "Call security. Call the police."

He made the calls and I sat at the foot of the bed, shaking, while David looked into the closet to satisfy his own curiosity.

Who knew Vacaar liked to cross-dress while practicing auto-erotic asphyxiation? Poor Vacaar! Caught red-handed, as it were, with his head in a plastic bag and his neck in a noose fashioned out of his own black leather belt.

Before I had run off screaming, a quick glance had confirmed the rumor that short men can be full of big surprises. No wonder Mona stuck to him like wallpaper. *Was that rigor mortis or was he that happy to be in Mona's shoes? Would she be more bothered by losing her Albanian stallion or by the fact that he had come and gone in her new Charles Jourdans?*

Chapter 21

Enderly and I waited in the living room until Wells and Koenig arrived. If I thought Enderly was on edge before this, now he was wound up like a chipmunk on coke. Nothing I could say would calm him. I could have used some calming myself. I clasped my hands together to keep them from shaking, but it didn't help.

Dave paced back and forth in front of the sofa, muttering to himself, until the two men arrived. He took them upstairs and I followed, standing near a corner of the bedroom, while the three men huddled in front of the closet doors. After a few moments, they moved into the bathroom to look around, so I went over to the closet. I had a ghoulish need to take another look at Luzi.

"Mrs. French, just what in tarnation do you think yer doin'?" Tom Koenig's voice boomed from behind me.

I jumped like a Florida sand flea. Was I disturbing the scene of a crime? I turned around, feeling guilty, though I had done nothing wrong.

"I—I'm sorry, Sergeant Koenig. I just had to see these shoes again. They're beautiful and I've never seen this particular style—"

He interrupted me with a peculiar look on his face, "Are you sayin' you've got a yen for those shoes? Well, you can forget about it. They are evidence," he said, enunciating each word of the last two sentences, as if he were speaking to a belligerent teenager.

"I do not have a yen for those shoes," I said, feeling indignant. "I merely have an interest in their design. They're far too large for my tiny little feet."

He looked down at my feet and relaxed a little. "Okay, but I still have a few questions for you and Mr. Enderly," and motioned for me to go back to the bedroom and sit.

While Rick called his investigative team, Enderly and I told Tom our stories—that we had been called to be here at 3:00 p.m. by Mr. Luzi himself. Koenig frowned and took a labored breath. If he would have had a gator tail to match his belly, it would have switched back and forth a few times, annoyed and menacing.

Tom didn't like me to begin with and, once again, here I was in the presence of a corpse. I had found the body without his help. It was like we were on an Easter egg hunt and my basket was more filled than his.

As I answered Koenig's questions, I wondered if Vacaar had killed himself by mistake or if he had been murdered. My first thought was that he had accidentally killed himself. I had read that this can happen in this dangerous sport.

But what if he had been murdered? What if the murderer had been hiding in the suite, waiting for his opportunity? Once Vacaar was on his knees in the closet with the belt around his neck, he was an easy target.

If it was a murder, why would someone kill Torrey, then Vacaar? They both liked the ladies. Maybe it was killers, plural. Maybe it was a band of angry women—angry at having been used and then dropped by these two overgrown adolescents, who always turned tail and ran back to their wives after the fun was over. Maybe Vacaar died a normal—okay, wiggy, freaky—death that involved no foul play whatsoever. What if it was a big old creepy coincidence and nothing more? On the other hand, maybe someone who knew about his proclivities set this scene up to make it *look* like a natural, sexual deviant's death. *Does such a thing exist?*

Once released from questioning, I said goodbye to David and trudged home in a stupor, not really seeing the marble sculptures nor the bromeliads on my path. I was deep in a ping-pong game in my head and I held both paddles. Was it murder? Was it accidental suicide? Was it Yin or was it Yang? Was everything black, white or striations of gray? Why Torrey? Why Luzi? I couldn't figure it out. My thoughts turned to French and the unfairness of it all.

"I want French. I need French, When are You going to deliver?" I asked aloud of God or the universe or my higher power or whoever was in charge. Someone once told me that praying out loud got speedy results. Did my words sound more like a demand than a request? Just to be safe, I muttered, "Please, thank You. Amen." and kept walking.

I was back at the house when the phone rang. It was Reed. "Great news, Maya!" he said.

"I am so ready for some great news, Doug. Lay it on me, baby."

"I got French out. He should be home in less than an hour."

Chapter 22

It had been over an hour now. No French. No call from French. Where the heck was he? I was tempted to call Doug to see exactly when he got French out of the Orange Avenue clink but decided against it. What would it help?

I sometimes felt like a pioneer woman, slogging along the ruts of the Oregon Trail, on foot next to my covered wagon. There was a train of wagons, there were women folk and kid folk. There were, of course, men folk. But my man, he was seldom with us in the ruts or around the campfire. No, he was one of the scouts. He was Meriwether Lewis French, blazing new paths, cutting back the undergrowth, chasing away the scary varmints for us, but not one to give a woman much steady company. I was often left to count the yellow blossoms on my plain, worn calico skirt and refasten the bow of my road-worn, muslin bonnet while other families huddled together over salted pork and little tins of heated beans.

Where is he, damn it? I felt taken for granted. I had been thinking exclusively of him, missing him, worrying about him when I was not trying to tease together the few clues I had to work with regarding—oh what was it again? Murder. He could at least call.

It was hard on me, flopping around alone in the house, waiting for French to come back. I boiled some water for tea and while I waited for it to brew, I sat at the piano and tinkered with a melody or two. I seldom played, but always told myself I should do it more often. Ugly thoughts popped into my head. *When did French get out of jail? In time to kill Luzi?* Then the doorbell rang.

I turned to look, but no one was there. It was hard to ring our bell and then just disappear. The double doors of the front entry were beveled glass. There were floor-to-ceiling glass transoms next to the doors. That made ten feet of glass, through which the path from the gate to the door could easily be seen.

Jumping up from the piano bench, I ran out the front door to double check. I looked left and right of the entry. No one. Just the water of the lake, mildly lapping at our grassy shore. *That's a little spooky.* I looked up the path for Rick's men. Where was a fake gardener when a girl needed one?

Seeing no one, I turned back to the house, and there, lying next to the door, was a plain brown box. It was wedged between one of the transoms and an oversized terra cotta planter.

I went inside, grabbed a pair of latex gloves and picked up the box. It was very light, neatly taped shut. I angled it toward the light to check for prints on the tape. There were none that I could see.

Back in the kitchen, I found a knife and opened the box. Nestled in white tissue paper was a typed note on expensive paper stock that read, "Maya, you have a run." Except someone had crossed out the "a" and printed the word, "to." There were also two boxes of L'eggs pantyhose. Size A. Suntan.

I examined the box and its contents carefully with my magnifying glass. No prints anywhere, not even on the shiny pantyhose cartons. Whoever did this was smart. Smart and careful. *Smart and Final.*

I walked to an overstuffed chair and placed my gift on the coffee table. I sipped my tea and contemplated the meaning of the gift and, while I was at it, the meaning of life.

Here I sat in the great room of a house on a fake lake in the middle of a luxury resort in Central Florida. People were turning up dead in the hotel. I kept turning up at the wrong place at the wrong time. My husband wasn't turning up at all. Swimmers, kayakers and wind surfers were gliding past this house, oblivious to the troubles of a few Sapphire executives, their wives and the Orlando Police Department.

None of it made any sense so why not do something nutty? Ancient peoples drank the blood of their enemies for courage and superior strength. Because it was the last thing anyone would expect, given the circumstances and the weather, I decided to wear one of the pairs of hose.

I had both legs in and was just pulling the sausage casing up to my waist when the phone rang.

David Enderly was on the line. "Is French there?" he asked.

"No. I thought maybe he went directly to the hotel after Reed got him sprung."

"No," he said, sounding haunted. "No one has seen him on property. Both Rick and Tom have been calling my office and paging me constantly. What do I tell them?"

"Tell them it's tea time. They need to sit down in the lobby, have some scones with jam and double Devon cream, some petit fours, a cup of Darjeeling and relax."

"Oh, yeah, right, Maya. That's not very helpful."

"Dave, it's all I've got." David was losing it. "If French comes to the house before he goes to the hotel, I'll have him call you."

"If he turns up here, I'll call you," Dave answered.

He sounded fissured. *For a guy with big ambitions, he's not handling the pressure of being Number One very well. Shouldn't I be more panicked than he? He's only missing a boss. I'm missing a husband and wearing pantyhose on a hot, sticky afternoon in Orlando.*

It was time for action. I decided to take my newly delivered gift box of L'eggs to Meeting Room C. Rick and Tom needed to see this.

Chapter 23

I was heading out the door when I noticed black skies overhead. Late afternoon and early evening storms were frequent in Central Florida. I paused under the overhang at my front doors. Should I continue on my errand or stay here?

My worst thinking said: *Go back inside, slip on your rain boots, grab an umbrella and make a dash for the hotel.*

My best thinking said: *Stay home a few minutes. This thing will pass through on a fast train.* Besides, the note had told me to run. Sometimes, it's good to take opposite action.

Orlando was located in the lightening strike capital of America. This strike zone fitted a broad sash from west to east, from Tampa to Melbourne. Lightening strikes in this zone often meant instant death. As a rule, it was tourists that were struck and killed because they somehow felt immune from tragedy while on vacation.

Thunder rumbled overhead and here I was, someone who knew better, eager to get to my destination, almost forgetting that staying inside for a while was a much better plan than risking my life for a handwritten note and some pantyhose boxes.

* * *

Wells and Koenig looked up from their desks as I entered. They were alone in the room. Their eyes swept over me, from toe to crown. They were none too subtle.

"What's up?" Rick said, looking at me like he saw a cockroach crossing the carpet.

"I've got something to show you guys," I said. "Look here." and I handed them the brown box and its contents. "Someone sent me a gift."

They opened it and looked inside.

Rick motioned to a chair in front of his desk. "Take a seat, Maya," he said.

"Don't mind if I do," I said and plunked myself down.

"Who sent you this note and the pantyhose?" Rick asked me.

I was silent a moment, then said, "You're kidding, right? How would I know who sent them? That's why I'm bringing them to you. Don't you have labs that can analyze this stuff?"

Rick shrugged and fiddled around with something on his desk, ignoring me. "Tom, put this stuff in a zip lock plastic baggie," he directed. Tom rummaged through some desk drawers, doing as he was told.

"I'd like the note back after you've had it analyzed, please," I said.

"Sure," Rick said. "Tom'll drop it by the house in a day or two."

No further conversation came my way so I asked, "What did the lab have to say about Vacaar Luzi?"

Rick and Tom looked at each other. Rick finally answered, "Mr. Luzi's neck was broken between vertebrae 2 and 3. The usual, in cases of autoerotic asphyxiation."

"So, then. No murder?" I asked.

"I didn't say that. I just said his death follows the usual pattern for this sort of thing." Rick seemed distracted.

I sat and wondered what was not being said.

"There was something unusual, however," Rick said, almost as an afterthought. "His forehead was bruised in an irregular, splotchy pattern not consistent with the angle at which his body lay on the closet floor."

"Sort of leaves things hanging, doesn't it?" I said, "if you'll pardon the expression."

They both glared at me, their eyes saying, "Please go."

"Well, it's been fun talking to you gentlemen," I said as I got up to leave. I was almost to the door, when Rick called out.

"When French decides to get back to this property, you'll be sure to let him know we're sitting right here, waiting to talk to him, won't you?"

"Oh yes, you can count on that," I told them.

* * *

Wouldn't you know? It had started again. The rain was coming down in diagonal sheets. I ducked around the corner from Meeting Room C and picked up a house phone.

"Dave, Hi! It's Maya. Have you heard from French?"

"No, ma'am. I'm waiting here for him with bells on." David sounded very tired.

David was a good hotelier, always making his best effort, but he seemed unprepared to be in charge of this entire property. And under these circumstances—not only 200 Sapphire Resort VIPs with the highest of expectation but now two of them were dead. His boss was playing hide and seek. *Where is French, anyway?* I asked myself for the hundredth time today. He had a lot of 'splaining to do when he got home.

David and I rang off and I went up the escalator to hang around the lobby until the cloudburst was over. The lobby was swinging. Soaked, giggling people ran in, shaking off the rain from their clothes and their shoes. The parrots on their stands bobbed their heads up and down, squawking and trilling. The high ionization of rainstorms always got them excited.

* * *

The squall ended and I was walking back home, purposely stepping in puddles with my rain boots, just to make a splash. I tore my mind from murder and pantyhose. I thought back to how French and I had met at the Sapphire Hotel on Sunset, ten years earlier.

Back then, he represented Sapphire Hotels and I represented myself, the sole proprietor of the tiny but profitable gift shop in the lobby. We negotiated my new lease, butting heads at every new clause. Eventually, my lease was renewed, the paperwork was signed. They say the anger section of the brain is positioned next to the love section at the base of the skull. I knew two people who met and argued in a hotel on the Sunset Strip during the music industry's golden days who would agree. A few months later, we signed our names on each others hearts.

When I looked up from my memories, I was at our garden gate. The moment I entered the house, my monkey mind was back to its preoccupation. Why had someone gone nutso and started killing Sapphire execs? Why was French still missing, when he should have been back hours ago? Why couldn't he at least call Dave and leave word for me, if he didn't have the courtesy to call me himself?

The phone rang. It was Rick. "The lab ran the production numbers of the pantyhose boxes. These two boxes came from Pennsylvania and went through distribution centers in Macon, Georgia and Ashland, North Carolina. The only prints on them were yours."

"What?" I said, startled. "How could that be? I wore latex gloves so I wouldn't leave prints."

"Dunno," said Rick. "When you hear from French, tell him that we just put out an APB on him. I hope he enjoyed his three hours of freedom."

Sometimes Southerners could really surprise you. They talked slow, they walked slow, they even seemed to think slow and yet, here they were, making my life miserable in double time.

Chapter 24

Frustrated, I didn't know what to do or where to go next. I paced across the travertine tiles in my entry. A fresh thought hit me. What if French had gone to see his good pal, Ted Rains, at Church Lane Depot, before returning to the hotel?

A few years back, Ted's professional reputation had survived the bad press of a murder in his entertainment complex in downtown Orlando. The murder had gone cold case but I had noodled around with the facts, as Ted had given them to me, and, within six months, I had solved the mystery. That was part of my history with Rick, Tom and the OPD.

That must be it—French was having a chat with Ted. But why had French not called me? On any normal day, he called me seven times, whether he needed to tell me something or not. Why then, when it was so important, did he not call me? I scratched my midriff, where the angry red welts were back for an encore.

I decided to pay Ted Rains a visit. It beat hanging around the house, waiting to hear from French while I scratched myself raw. I changed into some slacks and a top, grabbed my purse, my raincoat and my umbrella, in case of a new storm front, and walked to my car port. Ted Rains and Church Lane Depot were as good a place to start as any.

Obsessing over French, I was deep in thought as I put the key into my car door and only half registered the smell of a man's cologne. I liked that smell. Italian—maybe *Pino Silvestre*—it reminded me of Tuscany.

I had just asked myself why I was smelling *Pino Silvestre*, when someone grabbed me tightly at the waist, pinning my arms to my sides. I stiffened, then inhaled in terror and tore my mouth open in a scream. I struggled, pushing against him as I kicked and tried to wriggle loose from his iron grip. A thick, fleshy hand shoved a lumpy cloth over my nose and mouth. Now choking and gagging, I fought harder to break free. Instead, I went as limp as overcooked pasta. As the lights went out, I wasn't in Tuscany or even Florida anymore.

Chapter 25

I blinked and stared. Where was I? What time was it? I took stock before I moved. I was lying, face up, on hard ground. I wasn't in pain so long as I discounted the throbbing in my head. It felt like a tire iron being pounded into my gray matter by a framing hammer. I grabbed my skull and pressed down firmly, as though I were testing a cantaloupe for ripeness. My fingers searched for lumps, bumps or blood caked to my hair. None of the above, praise the Lord.

Cautiously, I sat up and noticed a dark green dumpster nearby. Warm blacktop pressed against my backside. I seemed to be missing one shoe.

Again, where was I? I cast my gaze farther about and then I got it. I was at the far end of a remote parking lot, with a tall, commercial building nearby that looked suspiciously like a hotel. It was loaded with sliding doors and balconies that had beach towels hanging over the railings.

This can't be one of French's properties, I thought, noting the sloppy towels. I stood, hoping I could keep my balance. I could and I hobbled forward a few steps, looking for my missing shoe. I found it and, a moment later, saw the words "Property of Sword and Chalice Hotel" stamped on the side of the dumpster.

So that's where I was! The Sword and Chalice was a fantasy-themed resort at Disney, about a mile from our Silver Pines.

I must walk into the Sword and Chalice and call someone for help— Lily. She would come get me. I brushed dust and debris off my clothes as I walked toward the hotel, still shaky. It was coming back to me. I had been on my way to see Ted Rains when someone had grabbed me. The thought shot a jigger of new pain and fear into my head and I felt nauseated, as I realized how vulnerable I had been and still was.

I walked as fast as I could across the blacktop and toward the glass entry doors. They opened wide for me. Once inside, I made a bee line across the lobby to the ladies' restroom. I looked in the mirror and tears sprang to my eyes. It wasn't that I looked so bad or that I was hurt. I was relieved to be in the hotel, safe in the restroom, but I was overcome with the knowledge of what might have happened to me. My hands were trembling and my legs felt like rubber.

I found the stand of pay phones and placed a collect call to Lily. Thank heavens for Lily. She said she'd drop everything and come get me. She didn't even ask for an explanation.

Lily lived a few miles away in Bay Hill, so I sat in a big, bamboo chair, facing the entry, to await her arrival. I wanted nothing more than to fade into the banana leaf pattern on the fabric of the cushions. I folded my still-shaking hands in my lap while I revisited what had happened to me.

"Why, Maya! Maya French, is that you?" a woman's voice trilled over the hum of the lobby crowd.

I felt defensive, but plastered a Sapphire Resorts smile on my face. "Margie, what a surprise! What are you doing here?"

"I was just about to ask you the very same thing!" It was Margie Enderly, David's wife, followed by her own little entourage of local, Sapphire Resort wives and a few assorted hausfraus. They were all dressed up for their girls' evening at Disney; their giddiness at being let out for the night gave them away.

Chapter 26

Lily pulled up at the front of the hotel in her black Range Rover. I popped up from my chair with as much elán as I could muster, wincing slightly as I raised my body from the deep cushions of the seat. Waiting had made me sore but, with a tiny sigh and a slow exhalation of breath, I walked up to the passenger side of her car.

Lily was chatting up the valets, pointing out that she needed no help as she was only picking up a friend, when I reached for the door to jump in.

"Not so fast, little darlin," a man's voice cooed over my shoulder and through my hair into my right ear, while his manicured hand covered my own on the door handle and gave it a little squeeze.

I knew that voice. I knew that hand. I knew that man. An old flame. I had hoped to avoid him. It was one of those unlikely twists of fate or a reverse miracle that brought this man to Orlando, Florida at the same time that the gods of my life had brought French and me here.

This man and I were more than friends when we both lived in Los Angeles. James had a high wattage personality and was a perfect fit with the Disney corporate culture.

"James, James, James—" I said, as I turned to look at him.

"You're not planning to leave just now, are you?" he asked, looking deep into my brown eyes with his own, while invading my personal space by nearly standing on top of me.

"Why, yes, James, I am," I said. "Lily just came by to pick me up. We're going out for a little jaunt."

"No, no. no," he said. He looked through the open car window at Lily and gave her a big, tanned smile full of perfect, white teeth. She knew about our past. She liked James. "I invite you both to stay. Why you're here to begin with, Maya, is no doubt a fascinating story, which I would love to hear."

"No, James. It's out of the question. We can't stay," I said.

"Un uh," James said, shaking his head, "I insist. Admit it. You have no particular plans. Let me show you our new Spa and Salon. French would want you to check out the competition," he added, flashing me his winningest grin.

"French knows there is no competition, James," I shot back.

"Still," he said. "I mean it. Come in, both of you. It will do you a world of good. Much better than whatever you thought you were going to do. I'm a great judge of these things, you know," he added. At the same time, he signaled to the valet to park Lily's car up front, in the VIP section. She would not be needing a claim ticket.

Lily got out of the car, amused at James, who was fawning all over me, while I gave him polite, monosyllabic brush-offs. The last thing on my wish list was a visit to a spa and salon. I wanted to pour my heart out to Lily—maybe even shed a melodramatic tear or two, while I had her sympathetic ear.

James insisted we stay and at least have a drink with him if we weren't going to the spa and, with an arm around each of our shoulders, he guided us to King Arthur's Royal Pub. Our drinks arrived and we toasted each other.

"Raise your glasses, girls," James said. "It's Mother's Day in Africa."

On the one hand, I was still edgy and eager to get out of there. On the other, it was comforting to be in the shelter of a reproduction British, medieval style, wood paneled bar that was all warmth, stained glass and soft lights. With Lily seated on one side of me and Mr. Big Booming Personality on the other, I felt safe.

I took a sip of hot Black Ceylon tea spiked with dark rum. Lily and James made small talk while I gazed at the array of exotic bottles behind the nearby bar.

"So, good looking," James said, turning to me, "How did you get here, anyway?"

I looked up and, with no warning, burst into tears. Lily reached for a napkin and pressed it into my left hand. James jumped from his seat and ran his fingers through his hair, mumbling, "What did I say? What did I say?"

In a minute, I composed myself and, sniffing, told them both my tale of woe. I cut it to a bare minimum and swore James to secrecy. There had been an in-house tragedy, French was now missing and I had been abducted.

"I'm calling the police," James said.

"You're doing no such thing," I told him. I might be wiping tears from my face but I was not letting James stick his nose into my life.

"They already know everything. They're on the case. They're got everything under control," I said.

"Like hell they do," James replied. "I've half a mind to call the FBI. I have friends there, Maya. You know that."

"Absolutely not, James. If you do something like that, I swear, I'll never speak to you again. Lily is my witness," I answered, pointing to her.

"If you think I'm going to sit here and do nothing, or maybe let Lily take you to your house or even hers, you are quite mistaken," he answered, in a huff.

"Let's enjoy a moment with each other and our drinks. We can discuss the other in a little while," Lily broke in, smiling, always the voice of diplomacy.

I pulled myself together and, despite the circumstances, we

spent a pleasant enough half hour together, with Lily and James deciding it would be best for Lily and me to stay here for the night, in one of James's unoccupied suites. His crack security team would be watching over us. It did sound better than going home alone to my empty house. Lily phoned William, her husband, and told him that I needed her; she was staying with me tonight.

James set everything up and, being James, began harping once again on his new spa. He insisted we go there now, be massaged and pampered so that we could relax, have room service in our suite afterwards, and get a good night's sleep.

I knew from experience, when James made up his mind, there was no point in trying to argue. We would be massaged, fed and then guarded in a top floor suite with all the bells and whistles. We would be as safe as gold bricks at Fort Knox. James would see to that.

Chapter 27

We had been acupressured and deep tissue massaged. Now, Lily and I sat together on chaise lounges made of teak. Bundled in thick, white Frette terrycloth robes after our showers, we sipped our herbal teas and regarded our fresh manis and pedis with some satisfaction, while we talked.

James had kept the spa open after-hours for us and it was heaven to be there with no other people or kids disturbing our peace and harmony. Kids were not allowed in hotel spas, anyway, for obvious reasons. Their presence added nothing positive to the atmosphere. A hotel spa was someplace women went in order to escape their children.

"Lily," I said, "I'm worried. It's not just that French is AWOL but also someone abducted me. What do you make of that?"

"Maya, I think you're in over your head. I think French knows something or is trying to track something on his own—"

I interrupted. "You don't think he's the murderer, do you?"

She looked at me with surprise. "What?" she whispered, as though the walls had ears. "You're again entertaining the notion that French could be the killer? Have you gone soft in the head?"

"Well, no," I answered, wiping at tears, confused and upset. "Of course not. I don't believe he could do it. No, that's not exactly true. I believe anyone could commit murder if the circumstances were right. But, do I think he did this? No. What would be his motive?"

"My point exactly," Lily agreed and reached over to give my hand a pat.

"Still, I think it's peculiar that he's disappeared. He has made no attempt to call me. I got abducted. Can you see where I'm coming from?"

"Of course, Duckie," she said, in her reassuring, Lily way. "Of course."

There was a brief silence. After a moment, I said, "Come on, let's go to our suite and get some sleep."

* * *

The next morning, I stopped by James's office and left a thank you note with his secretary. He was in a meeting. Great! We could sneak off without a big scene.

Wrong. As Lily and I walked from the lobby to her parked car, James trotted up and hailed us, giving Lily an air hug and then turning to me.

"I'm sorry you're leaving, Maya," he said, almost tearing up. "Stay safe, you promise?" He was big with tearing up. That was one of the reasons I had to leave him. I couldn't stand the moisture.

He hugged me fully. Right there in front of God and Lily and everyone in the circular driveway. The man had no shame.

I pushed away from him. "Thank you for your generosity, James. You're a good friend."

"Any time, Maya," he said, perhaps realizing he had hugged me a bit too tightly. He walked us to the car, opening first my door, then Lily's. His heart was in the right place even if other parts of him were a bit out of line. For example, there was that flagpole in his custom made, gabardine trousers. I wondered how he would make it back to his office without some tourist draping a soggy beach towel over it.

Chapter 28

As we left the wonderful world of Disney, Lily drove north on Apopka-Vineland Road and I asked to use the little notebook I knew she kept in her purse.

"Sure, Maya," she said, lifting her purse from the floor of the seat behind me and plopping it in my lap. "Just dig around till you find it and a pen."

I began to dig as instructed and, before I found the pen and notebook, I noticed something shiny in her bag. *Odd. Isn't this identical to that weird shiny thing we saw in Vacaar Luzi's bathroom drawer? Or maybe it is that weird shiny thing. Why would Lily have one of those or why would she have taken it from that drawer?*

My digging must have slowed to mere scratching because Lily looked over at me and asked, "What's the matter, Duckie? Not having any luck? I know they're in there somewhere."

"Oh, I'm still looking," I said and wondered—if this shiny gadget were Lily's, why had she acted as though she had never seen one before? Was Lily not to be trusted? A slight queasiness struck me and my mouth felt dry. I swallowed and said nothing.

"Found them!" I declared triumphantly, extracting the pen and paper from her purse. My suspicion made me prickly and my midriff began to itch. What next? I was already having my doubts about French and now this. My world was shattering like a broken mirror, and me without my Crazy Glue.

"I want to jot some notes," I told her, opening the pad and uncapping the pen. "Let's see. First, find French and strangle him..."

"At least you still have your sense of humor, sweetness," Lily smiled and kept her eyes on the road.

"You know what," I said, "I've given up on French. He's going to turn up when he decides to turn up. It wouldn't be the first time he's disappeared only to reappear later with a perfectly reasonable story."

"But never under these circumstances," Lily said.

"No. Never under these circumstances," I agreed.

"Back to my list," I said, determined to get my mind off French. "One, I need to figure out why Lauren White was still at the hotel so late that very first night. Two, I should probably interview some of the guys who were at the dinner dance, like Frankie Messina. Three, I need to examine the files in French's office. Four, I need to look through our Visa bills to see if French really did purchase any pantyhose lately. Finally, I should talk to Mel, the Weinstein in charge of Sapphire Resorts, to see if he can shed any extra light on the personal lives of Redmund Torrey and Vacaar Luzi."

"Do you think Rick will let you do any of that stuff without tailing you?" Lily asked me.

"No, probably not," I admitted. "But I've got to try. If I have to break into French's office at four in the morning, I will." I knew there was a secret way into his office that probably even the Orlando PD had not discovered.

Lily and I decided not to return to Silver Pines just now. After all, I was sprung from lock-down mode and the snooping eyes and ears of all the good and bad people on the property, including Rick, his henchmen, at least one murderer and a kidnapper.

Chapter 29

Lily and I stopped at the Gateway Shopping Center. It was breakfast time and Tammy's Cafe was a great local joint for a bite. Tammy made omelets like no other. They seemed lighter than air, yet bursting with flavor. How did she do it? She refused to tell anyone. Talk on the streets was that even her employees didn't know her secret.

We sat at the counter, Lily and I, lost in our thoughts while we chowed down our veggie and cheese omelets. Tammy baked her own biscuits, also lighter than air. They were so good, they almost seemed like dessert. In front of us, Delbert, our server, his back turned, was busy rinsing out glasses in hot water. The steam rose in curls around him. *If I had a job like that, my hair would be a constant ball of frizzy twine.*

"Why would someone abduct me, Lily," I asked her, still looking at Delbert.

"I don't know, Maya. Did you ever stop to think it might be a message to keep the hell away from the murders?" she asked.

"That thought *did* occur to me," I admitted, "but I struck it immediately. You and I both know that's not going to happen."

"No, of course not," she said, looking with either pity, disapproval or maybe even wistful protectiveness at her dear, knuckle-headed friend.

"Not to revisit an unpopular subject, but what do you suppose has happened to French?" she ventured, watching for my response with her smart, hazel eyes.

"Beats me," I answered. "That man can be so vexing at times. He's so independent, I sometimes wonder why he bothered to get married." I noted her look of surprise. Seldom did I let down my guard regarding French, allowing even a sliver of my frequent frustrations with him to show.

Just then, some men entered and slid into a booth against the wall. Our backs were to them. Lily and I perked up. We both recognized the voices and were ready to eavesdrop with the best of them.

"This whole deal has thrown me for a loop," said Rick.

"You said it," Koenig answered. "Do you think we should call in the state troopers to help us with this?"

"Absolutely not," Rick said. "We can handle this. It's the biggest thing to come our way, ever. When we solve these murders, we're not going to share the glory with any other department or bureau."

"How long can we keep those Sapphire conference people caged up on the property?" Tom asked. "Life goes on and we have to release them back to theirs sooner or later."

"You're right, but everything's too fishy. I don't like that French has disappeared and I don't like that nosey Maya snooping around. She's a piece of work, isn't she?" Rick answered.

Lily and I hunched over our plates. Now was not the time to be found out. I was trying to blend into the stainless steel countertop and the red Naugahyde of the bar stool. Chances were we were safe from discovery. If they hadn't noticed us yet, they probably weren't going to.

"Yeah," Tom said. "Something's got to be done about her."

"Like what?" Rick asked.

"Maybe we can trump up some charges against her, set her up for a fall. We can put her in jail to get her out of our hair,"

Tom said.

I couldn't believe what I was hearing. They had nerve to speak about this in public. I guess they reckoned no one was listening. I guess they were wrong.

Now I had one more thing to worry about—them. Part of me had been wondering if Rick had somehow finagled my abduction to give me pause. The answer was no.

Truth was, whoever abducted me knew exactly what he was doing. The intent was to scare me away from the case. He could have easily dumped me into the nearest body of water.

In Florida, it was easy to do away with a corpse, if one just happened to have a corpse lying around. The woods that flanked the Interstate were swampy and bordered by lakes or maybe the lakes were bordered by woods and swamps. From an airplane, Central Florida looked like soggy Swiss cheese surrounded by oversized parsley.

Those woods, swamps and lakes were stocked with nature's clean-up crew, the crew of wide snouts, strong jaws and jagged, alligator teeth. A body could be dropped off at midnight and, by morning, no evidence would remain.

My thoughts returned to Lily and how we were trapped at the counter. I motioned to Delbert, placing my finger over my mouth to signal he should be quiet. He jerked his head up silently, telling me he understood, and bent his head in near to us to hear what I was going to say.

"We'll have dessert," I said to him. "Why don't you grab us a piece of cherry pie and two forks," I said, nodding toward Lily, who was as silent as a meadow mouse. "And Delbert, don't say our names."

"Okay, you two," he said and nodded. "Would you like that à la mode?"

"Of course, dear Delbert," I said, keeping my voice low. "If we're going to hell in a hand basket, it may as well be worth our while."

Chapter 30

I had pictured Lily and myself sneaking out of Tammy's, after Rick and Tom ate their meal and left. We would dart into Walgreen's together, where I wished to make a purchase. Then, Lily would bring me back to the hotel property via Winter Garden Road and drop me off at the gravel path where our Fire Station stood. The hunky firemen would wave at me and their friendly Dalmatian, Domino, would trot by my side for a while, then turn and go back to the station where he belonged.

It would already be noon and the air would be fragrant with the scent of the pines and the sweet acacia that grew wild on the property.

Normally, I walked along, breathing that sweet air, not a care in the world. But not today. Today, once Lily dropped me, I would be alone, scared, missing French, and at the same time, hoping he might have turned up last night or this morning, while I was away. I would also be looking over my shoulder every step of the way, since I seemed to be sporting my own private stalker.

But no. As it turned out, I rode home in the back of Rick's Grand Victoria cruiser. It smelled a little of dog.

"Well, as I live and breathe." Rick's voice had rung out as he paid his check. "It's Maya French and her friend, Lily!"

We were caught. What could we do but swivel on our stools, smile with cherry-stained teeth and greet him in return?

"Would you like a ride home, Maya?" Rick asked.

"No thank you, Rick. Lily's got it covered."

"No, really. I insist," he said. Then, to Lily, "You get along home now—we've got it from here."

Lily didn't argue with Rick and I didn't, either. She was driving back to Bay Hill alone. We gave each other an air kiss and parted ways in the parking lot, where she hightailed it to her Range Rover, while I followed Rick and Tom to their car.

I slid into the back seat and sniffed the air. "I didn't know this was a canine unit!" I exclaimed in surprise.

Rick and Koenig shot each other an irritated glance.

"It's not," Rick said.

"Oh, come on now. Don't be coy, gentlemen," I said. "I can smell Lassie in here. Where do you hide the Milkbones?" I was already in deep doo-doo for having left the property without their permission, that much was obvious, so why not get further under their skins?

Rick's eyes, slitty and mean-looking, were visible to me in the rear view mirror.

"Very funny, Maya," he said.

About as funny as a dead armadillo in the middle of the road.

Koenig burped loudly, didn't even try to excuse himself. Hard to excuse a guy like him. He must have sensed it.

"Why were you off property?" Rick asked in an accusatory tone.

"It wasn't really my choice, Rick."

"And that means—"

"Someone abducted me and schlepped me to the back of the Sword and Chalice property," I answered.

"At Disney? What on earth for?" I saw Rick's jaw working silently.

"How should I know?"

He was silent for a moment while he thought it over. Koenig stared at him like a dog waiting for a command from his master. Maybe that accounted for the smell in the car.

"When were you going to tell us this?" Rick finally asked.

"I don't know." I looked down at my lap, feeling a tiny bit guilty. I had never intended to mention it to them at all and Rick knew it.

Koenig made a disgusted, snorting sound and burped once more. The rest of the ride was awkward.

As they dropped me at the path which led to my home, Rick yelled after me, "Keep yourself put on this property, Maya. It's for your own good."

"You're right, Rick. Thanks for the ride, I appreciate it," I said, waving goodbye.

When I got inside the house, the red light on my phone was flashing. I listened to the message. It was from French. French! French was alive! French had called me. A wave of relief and joy shot through me, very soon followed by a wave of annoyance and an urge to thwock him upside the head.

That insensitive moron. Did he have any idea how worried I had been about him? And what was worse, his message said almost nothing. He told me he was fine and not to worry. He didn't want to stay on the line. He didn't want the police tracing the call. I, too, suspected surveillance. It was just a feeling I had.

I played the message over and over again, listening for any sort of encrypted code or stress in French's voice. Was someone holding a knife to his throat or a gun to his head? That could make a person terse, all right.

But no, there was no trace of panic or untoward emotion in his voice. He was checking in to calm my fears. No mention of where he was or when he would be back. So many questions and not one answer. Once again, I wanted to jump in my car, bolt from the property and drive up to see Ted Rains. As French's closest friend in Orlando, he might be able to shed some light on this madness.

The last time I tried that, I woke up near a dumpster behind the Sword and Chalice hotel over at Disney. So, I called Ted and requested he have someone come collect me at the property.

"Maya, darlin', I'll be happy to do that. It will be about half an hour. I'll have my man, Marty, ring the bell at the gate to your property. You know Marty, don't you?" Ted's voice was quiet, calm, soothing—and he hadn't even asked me why I needed a driver.

True to Ted's word, Marty arrived half an hour later. I jumped into the limo in clean, flax-colored linen slacks, the matching linen jacket folded carefully over my arm.

Chapter 31

"Maya, so good to see you and don't you look lovely," Ted said, as he rose from his desk and came around to give me a big, friendly hug.

"Thank you, Ted," I answered. "How's Lisa?"

"Prettier than ever," he said. "She's been asking about you. You two should go water skiing sometime on our lake."

"Sure thing," I answered, thinking that would never happen. Lisa had known me for three years and never invited me to anything.

I was not good at small talk. "Ted, I need some help," I blurted.

"Have a seat, darlin', What can I do?" he answered, grinning at me in that gentle, Southern way of his.

"First off, have you seen French today?"

"Why, yes, I have," he answered, smiling into my eyes.

"Oh, thank goodness!" I exhaled and leaned back in the leather chair. "That is such music to my ears, you have no idea," I continued. "Is he all right?"

"He's fine, Maya."

"Is he still here, somewhere on your property?" Church Lane Depot was big—a block of historic buildings, all turned into saloons, restaurants, game arcades, antique shops and even a boutique hotel.

"No, he left about an hour ago," he said.

"Can't you tell me everything? I feel like we're playing twenty questions." Ted was a nice guy, a good friend, and I didn't want my impatience to show. But my mask of calm was beginning to melt and slip down the edges of my cheeks.

"I can't tell you everything," Ted said. "I promised. But I can tell you," he continued, "that he's fine. He asked me to buy him some new clothes, which I did. He took a shower and borrowed a car. I don't know where he went, but he did leave a note for you, just in case you came around. Seems he knows you pretty well." He handed me a sterling silver letter opener and an envelope. I ripped it open on the spot.

"Don't look for me, Maya, and don't worry about me," it read. "Go home. Relax. I'm following a lead. I'm not in any danger. Love you ever, French"

Go home. Relax. Was he kidding? Did he think I would head home now, sashay over to the pool and grab a Tequila Sunrise?

My meeting with Ted was over. Was I relieved, deflated or confused? A little of each.

Ted invited me to walk over to the main room of the Church Lane Saloon with him, to listen to his new fiddler, Chet Watkins. I agreed, in order to be polite. Ted and I ordered sparkling water and toasted to French's health.

We sat on wooden benches near the rafters of the great brick warehouse turned concert venue and dance hall, looking down at Chet. Chet was burning up the strings of his fiddle, playing "The Devil Went Down to Georgia".

After the last resounding chord, we stood up to leave. Ted walked me to the limo, where Marty was waiting. I thanked Ted and waved goodbye, as we pulled away from the curb.

I leaned back and thought about the devil in Georgia. With dead bodies strewn around and abductions on the rise, I was fairly convinced he had made a detour to Florida and was cruising around Orlando just about now.

Chapter 32

Safely deposited back at the main entrance of the hotel by Marty, I walked through the glass entry doors. I was hit by a blast of air conditioning as cold as a Klondike bar. I ran into Lauren White, running, as usual, from point A to point B in high heels and a short skirt.

"Where are you off to now?" I asked.

"You know how it is, Maya. Usually, it's French who keeps me running. Now that he's not here, it's Dave. He's got me watching everyone at the conference. It's my job to keep them occupied and happy. I'm busier than a one-armed paper-hanger."

I chuckled. "It must agree with you," I said, "You look great!" And she did. Lauren was one of the beautiful people. She was single and looking for "the" man. I could have seen her as a threat but, being a good Southern girl from a fine Southern family, a married man would never have been the man for her.

Lauren and I said goodbye and then I wondered, why go back to my home on the lake? I knew what awaited—an empty house full of shadows. The palmetto bugs and wood spiders might miss me if I stayed away a while longer, but they were the only ones.

I thought about French's note to me. I should go home and

relax. But I couldn't do that yet. Instead, I walked over to the lobby bar with its raised, white, concert grand piano on a revolving stage, and sat down in one of the basket-style loveseats. They were meant for two but it was just Maya French, alone, as usual. I sat toward the back, unnoticed, and took in my surroundings.

I mentally reviewed the events of the previous three days and nights: someone had wrung Redmund Torrey's neck on Friday night, just after the Sapphire Hotels and Resorts national management shindig had begun—changing the tone of the conference just a teensy bit for those of us in the know. An incriminating receipt had been planted in French's office and he had been trotted off to jail. It had been a plant, hadn't it? Between the receipt, the pantyhose box on his desk and his disappearing act, I was confused and uneasy in so many ways.

Sometime the next afternoon, Vacaar Luzi was swept off his wife's sexy Charles Jourdan's and iced. French had been released from jail but was still MIA.

On my way to see Ted Rains at Church Lane Depot, someone had slipped a chloroformed hankie over my nose and mouth and taken me for a little spin. When I came to on Disney property, I called Lily to come get me, we ran into James, the hotel director there, and he made us stay in a suite at his hotel overnight. The next morning, Lily and I went to Tammy's for an omelet. Then, I was escorted home by Rick and a belching Koenig, his burps almost making me rolf.

Next, I changed clothes and made it to Ted's place and back. At least I knew French was alive and well. Now, I was sitting in the lobby piano bar with a stiff upper lip and a Gold Cadillac, which looked like it was going to be my dinner.

Pretty much, I knew nothing and I was getting no smarter sitting here. I thought about all the people I knew at Sapphire and wondered which of them had been closest to Torrey. Would there be any sense in trying to question them? How long could the OPD and our staff keep this whole mess quiet?

My mind doubled back to French, as it always did. Where the hell was he? Always traipsing off when I needed him most. Someday, when this was all a distant memory, I would have to pull a disappearing act on him, just one time, just to get even. Would he even notice?

Chapter 33

"Hi there, may I sit with you?" A woman's soft voice broke my train of thought.

I looked up and into the lake blue eyes of Alana Torrey, grieving widow number one. I nodded, smiled and scooted to one side of the loveseat. She sat her slender self into the other side and there was still room to spare between us. If the rich were indeed different, then so were the beautiful. On my brightest and best day, I would never be an Alana Torrey.

Alana embodied my ideal of feminine everything. A cross between a Barbie doll and an expert on international business, she was also a style queen, who must have catalogued her clothes and kept detailed records of what she wore when, where and with whom, as she never wore the same ensemble twice.

Along with her now-dead husband, Alana had always been the public face of Sapphire Resorts, frequenting the society pages of magazines such as *Town and Country*, *Vogue* and *Vanity Fair*. I wondered if designers comped her ball gowns for high profile events. She was seated right next to me, probably looking for companionship and compassion, or maybe she even had a confession to make—and I was busy envying her.

"Alana, I've been worried sick about you," I lied, remembering how my thoughts had been consumed with French, the murders and Alana not at all.

"I've stayed in my suite this whole time. It's strange. It feels like time has stopped. I feel empty. Everything feels unreal, like I'm observing from a distance."

"Oh, Alana—" I said. There were no words. Looking into her sad, tired eyes, my self-absorbed little heart *did* go out to her and I teared up a little with her.

The cocktail server arrived, breaking the mood, and took Alana's order, a champagne cocktail. Interesting choice. Something ticked in my brain. Champagne? Wasn't that usually reserved for celebrations?

We sat together, listening to Harry Parker on the piano. That man could play anything from Rachmaninov to Luther Vandross. No matter what state anyone's state was in, music could transport people to better times and better places.

Her drink arrived and Alana raised her glass to me before she took her first sip. "Here's to us," she said, her eyes fixed on some point in the distance. "One of us, the usual Sapphire widow, whose absentee husband is farting around this property somewhere; the other, a *real* Sapphire widow, whose husband won't be farting at all any more. Campai!"

Wow! I had not expected such a pithy toast from her. It only went to show that you couldn't judge a lady by her persona, her footwear or her designer togs. There might be a lot more to Alana than I had ever guessed. I clinked glasses and wondered if a petite dolly like her had the muscle to toss a two-hundred pounder down a laundry chute.

We sipped together in silence for a moment, then she turned to me with a sigh and said, so very softly that at first I thought I had heard wrong, "I knew about all of Red's other women, of course."

"That must have been difficult for you," I said, hoping my shock didn't show.

"Oh, it was. It sure was. Redmund was not easy."

What could I say? I nodded dumbly and took another sip of my drink.

"He was hard to live with," she said, almost to herself. I turned my gaze toward her and looked into her eyes, so near, so transparent, so blue.

"Hard to live with, all right, but I never would have guessed this." She paused. "Turns out, he's much harder to live without."

I nodded solemnly. What was I to make of this? She loved him and missed him, in spite of his character defects? Or, was it regret? Did she wish she had not strangled him now that he was gone? I took another sip of Gold and maintained my silence.

My mind wandered off to pantyhose. What would be Alana's preferred brand? Just then, she crossed her long, blonde legs and I looked down. She was wearing no hose at all.

Chapter 34

Alana finished her champagne and left. My Gold Cadillac came to its inevitable end. I sat for a moment, wondering what to do. I still didn't feel like going back home. I dreaded it, the uncomfortable solitude, the not knowing where French was nor why he refused to come home. Heck, if he didn't want to be there, why would I? No, I sat there in my little loveseat, all alone, unloved and unlovable, feeling like Little Bo Peep, who had not just lost her sheep but had lost her way.

I know—I'll pop into the accounting department to see if Jake might still be in the office. We can have a chat.

I heard Jake before I saw him. He was on the phone and laughing about something. What did accounting execs have to laugh about on their office phones? Bookings were up at the hotel. Maybe that alone would be enough to make a bean counter laugh.

He looked up and waved me in, still cradling the phone to his ear with his left shoulder and pushing the buttons of an electric adding machine perched in the middle of his desk.

"Maya, my love, what's up?" he asked, as he hung up the phone.

"I'm all mixed up, Jakey dear. I can't find French. No one can find French. I don't know what to do."

"Hmm," he said. "What else?"

"Well, someone tried to kidnap me."

"*What?*" Jake said, pinpointing me with his slate blue eyes.

"Yeah. That was strange," I answered.

"That was *strange*? That's all you can say?" he barked.

"Gee, you don't have to sound so mean," I said. "Remember, it happened to me once before, back at the Sapphire on Sunset, in a previous life."

"Oh yeah, I forgot about that," he answered, looking up at the air, and paused. "Were you bound and gagged this time, too?"

"No. This time I was dumped outside the Sword and Chalice. Weird, huh?"

"Do you suppose that slimeball, James, did it?" he asked.

"What, and possibly get a wrinkle in his pressed gabardines? I think not," I said and we both had a laugh at James's expense.

Jake's voice turned serious. "Maya, I don't want you wandering around alone any more. It's too dangerous. Sure, Rick has his men everywhere but where were they when you were abducted? How could that even happen?"

"I don't know," I answered quietly. That had been bothering me, as well.

"I'm leaving my office in a few minutes," Jake said. "I want you to wait here while I finish up. Then, I'm personally walking you to your house and making sure it's safe. I won't leave until I know you're locked inside."

"Thanks, Jake," I said. "I'll meet you at the gift shop. I need to buy a new pair of pantyhose for tonight. I promise I'll stay right there."

He looked at me, weighing the possibilities. "I don't know whether I can trust you to stay put," he said, cocking his head to one side. "You understand this is serous, right?"

"Yes," I said, putting my right hand up in the air. "Scout's honor. I'll stay put. No worries. See you there!" With that, I turned and left, heading to the lobby gift shop.

Chapter 35

There is a rhythm to a hotel. Busy in the morning, fairly quiet until lunch. After lunch, quiet again until the late afternoon, when all the happy campers return from Happy Valley, hauling bags of souvenirs, gifts for the folks back home and, most likely, a stuffed animal or two. They hang around, swapping stories, in the hotel lobby for a while.

The gift shop at Silver Pines was much larger than most hotel gift shops. It was divided into four sections: menswear, women's wear, sundries and even a grocery section. Quite a few hotel guests were shopping. People were in from their day tours to Disney, Universal Studios and Cypress Gardens and they had not yet gone to eat at one of our dining outlets or returned to their rooms.

I had already made my purchase and was now killing time, browsing through the magazines, when I thought I recognized someone in the women's section. I saw the back of Alana Torrey's head. She was talking to David Enderly and a woman who looked familiar. It was hard for me to get a good view of them; too many shoppers between us.

I wove my way through the people and the displays, the clothing racks and the busy errant children, who were touching everything with their pudgy little sticky fingers. I wanted to eavesdrop on Alana—what could she, David and Linda Messina have to say to one another that was so important that their heads were bowed together, as if they were telling secrets in third grade?

I stumbled over a toddler. He yelped and I shrank behind a greeting card display, while mumbling, "I'm sorry, I'm sorry," to both the little boy, who started to sniffle, and to his mother. Mom turned toward me, shooting daggers with her eyes, while she comforted her son.

My only thought: *Did I blow my cover?* It seemed not. Unaware of their surroundings, Alana, David and Linda continued to talk. Their eyes were locked, and their facial expressions were serious, even tense. I continued to edge closer, hiding behind a large round rack of women's sweat suits, thumbing through the clothing as though I were looking to buy.

"What do you mean?" I heard Alana say, in a tone of hushed surprise.

"Just what I said," Linda responded. "I know what I saw."

"Linda," Alana answered, "I think you should keep this to yourself. You don't know whom this could harm if this came out."

"Okay," she answered with reluctance, her left hand crinkling the fabric of her tennis shorts. "I better go now." She gave Alana one last glance before she moved away.

"This will all work out for the best. You'll see," Alana called after her.

David had said nothing during the conversation, only nodded his head once in a while, as though he were committing every word to memory.

Alana then headed out the doors toward the elevator lobby and David and Linda headed briskly in the opposite direction toward the sculpture garden.

At 6:30 p.m., why would Linda be heading out with David at her side? She was supposed to go to her room to change for a Sapphire dinner event on the mezzanine level. I knew this because I was supposed to be doing that same thing.

It was too irresistible. I had to snake through the loitering guests and follow them. Jake would understand when I called him later and explained my thinking. Jake might play at it but he could never stay angry with me for long.

Chapter 36

Linda and David were walking through the sculpture garden, when David tripped over something and almost fell. I was afraid Linda might see me as she turned and asked if he was all right, but they continued their walk toward Papa's. A moment later, David looked at his pager, said goodbye to Linda, and hurried off toward the pool.

Was Linda going to have a drink with her husband, Frankie, before cleaning up and heading to the dinner? It could be, I supposed. I was beginning to feel foolish for following her when she, abruptly, made a 180° turn and began walking toward me.

"Well, hello, Maya! How nice to run into you here. Are you going to meet French for a drink?" she asked.

"Actually, I was just going to use the little girls' room," I lied. "It's one of the best on the property and underused this time of day."

"I have to go, too," she said. "Mind if I join you?"

I wanted to say, "Oh, great!" Instead, I said, "That would be fine, Linda. Friends that tinkle together, winkle together."

She looked at me, as if to say, "Huh?" and then laughed. "Maya, you are such a card!" she said, and off to the restroom we strolled.

Once outside of Papa's again, we took leave of one another. She said she was headed back to her room to change. I wasn't so sure but I couldn't follow her again. My chance to spy on her had passed. Frustrated, I walked away from her toward my home.

In the restroom, she had mentioned nothing about her chance meeting with Alana and David in the gift shop, but why would she? She also didn't mention why she was headed to Papa's Place, then decided against it. I wanted to ask her but it was none of my business.

As I took the shortcut on the hanging bridge over the pool toward home, I pondered these things. I was in the middle of the hanging bridge, walking as briskly as a person who is swaying from side to side can do, when I heard a popping sound. At once, my left shoulder stung worse than the time a deer fly bit me. When I checked it out, my linen jacket seemed to be oozing grenadine. Then, darkness closed in like a collapsing umbrella and I sank where I stood, swaying slightly, twenty feet above the deep end of the pool.

Chapter 37

I was awakened by the smell of bacon. Gosh, was it breakfast time already? I hoped so. I was ready for waffles, smothered in butter and maple syrup. I started to get up.

Ouch! It was not time to get up. I was in a world of hurt and in a moving vehicle. Everything was a little fuzzy, but as I turned my head, I saw a good-looking kid sitting next to me, sinking his teeth into a double-bacon cheese burger. That explained the smell of Saturday morning breakfast, but why was I lying here next to a teen-ager in uniform?

Then I remembered. That popping noise. My shoulder. My linen suit. "Is my suit ruined?" I tried to say to the hungry kid but all that came out was a garbled slur of brain salad. He removed the burger from his face, adjusted something at my side, and told me to rest.

The next time I woke up, I was still fuzzy and now in a hospital bed. Two men were talking in low tones nearby. I turned my head and squinted to my left. It looked like Jake and Dave Enderly, seated on chairs next to me.

I coughed, then said, "Hey guys, what are you doing here?"

They popped up from their seats. David handed me a teddy bear.

"Here, this is for you. You could have been killed, Maya," he said, sounding more accusatory than sympathetic. His face looked haggard and his color wasn't good.

"Thanks," I said, taking the teddy in my arms. "You don't look well."

"I don't feel well, thank you. I've got a lot on my mind, but I had to come here to make sure you were all right."

"I'm the one who found you, dangling on the bridge over the pool," Jake broke in.

"What?" I didn't remember that.

"Yeah, you were just hanging around—" he said and laughed.

"Ha, ha. Very clever," I said.

Dave looked anxious. "Maya, I've got to get back to the hotel. Get well and hurry back, okay?"

"Okay, David. Thanks for the teddy," I said and he left.

Jake was filling me in on what had happened and how he had called the paramedics, when he stood up and said, "You have a visitor. I think I'll go stretch my legs for a moment."

He left and another man entered. "Hello, Beautiful!" The bright hospital lights silhouetted his frame in the doorway and my grogginess made my vision a little dimmer than usual.

"French?" I said, "Is that you?" For a split second, my heart dared to hope. I felt a shudder of comfort and joy inside of me. But, as I focused, I realized it was only James. Not that it wasn't nice to see him but, considering the circumstances, I would have preferred to see French. Poor James always came in second. He always placed, but never won.

He approached me with his left hand behind his back and, with a flourish, he presented me with a bouquet of roses, pink Gerber daisies, dianthus and freesia. He had remembered my favorites.

I took a deep breath. Ahhh, it was nice to feel loved even if it wasn't by the right guy.

"Thank you, James," I said. "How did you know I was here? I didn't know I was here."

"Good news travels fast," he said and paused for drama, "but bad news travels even faster."

He drew a chair up close to me, sat down and took my left hand gently in his. "Does it hurt when I hold your hand?" he asked with such sincerity in his puppy dog, brown eyes that I almost remembered what I had loved best about him. I felt a wee bit guilty, but his attention was giving my spirits a boost.

Jake came back just then, saw us holding hands and cleared his throat. "So, James, just so super to see you," he said, and they shook hands.

"Here, Jake. Be a good guy and find a vase for these, will you?" James said, handing over the bouquet. Jake looked at me and rolled his eyes but, nonetheless, did as James asked.

The two Js in my life had a long standing mutual dislike for each other. I hoped this visit wouldn't give Jake the wrong idea about James and me.

After a short while, I told James I was tired and needed to rest. He took the hint, promising to look in on me again, to see how I was doing.

Jake returned and set the vase on the window sill. "What was that jackal doing sniffing around here, Maya? You haven't taken up with him again, have you?"

"What?" I said, surprise and reprimand heavy in my voice. "You surely know better than that."

He gave me a strange grin. I got the idea he didn't believe me.

"You know what?" he said, "when you get out of here, I'm going to stay with you until French gets back. You can't talk me out of it, so don't try. I don't like any of this. None of it. You need a keeper, Maya."

What could I say? I winced pitifully, and gazed into his appraising blue eyes with adoring gratitude.

"Jake," I said, "you're my hero. What would I do without you?"

Chapter 38

It was Wednesday morning. Jake had brought me home from the hospital last evening, still mildly sedated. I had slept off the drugs and realized I had no idea what was going on with French, the murder investigation, or the world, in general, but I was itching to get back out there amongst them. Jake knew me well. He took the day off just to keep me in his sights at home. There was no hope of escape.

He had called Lily earlier and she was wandering around my house, as well. They were relaxed, knowing that even though my shoulder had been only grazed, I was in no shape to jump off my deck or crawl through a bathroom window to give them the slip. As I cleaned up and got dressed, I could hear their animated conversation coming from the kitchen.

I had missed Monday night's conference supper and all of yesterday's events. Every meeting I did not attend was a lost opportunity to find the murderer or murderers. There wasn't a whole lot left of the Sapphire conference. In a few days, the visiting execs would be straggling off our property and heading back to their own resorts and hotels. So many opportunities to observe my list of suspects were gone, and I was missing a valuable one right now. Added to the pain in my left shoulder, I was feeling grumpy, out of sorts and, therefore, not exactly good company.

I was resting on my bed, feeling sorry for myself when the doorbell rang. I heard Jake open the front door and welcome Rick Wells and Tom Koenig. I put on my happy face, exited the bedroom, and greeted my guests.

They told me they were sorry to see me laid up like this— they now had an extra detail devoted to just me, security had been beefed up, etc., etc. Oh, sure.

For a moment, I entertained the thought that they might have shot me themselves to keep me out of the action. Truth was, I had gotten on somebody's nerves, someone who wanted me out of the picture more than even Rick and Tom did. Was it the same somebody who had dragged me to the Disney dumpster three days ago? So much had happened that it seemed like half a lifetime ago. And then there was the issue of my missing husband, Mr. Hubert French.

"Maya, as you probably realize," Rick's voice interrupted my musings, "the Sapphire conference is drawing to a close. It was impossible to keep the lid on this thing any longer, so, while you were in the hospital, we interviewed the top tiers of visiting execs to get their statements. So far, the crime lab has come up empty. There are no fingerprints, no lipstick marks on glasses, no shoe prints, nothing. Whoever the murderer is, he knows his stuff. He may have killed before. In fact, we may be looking at murder for hire."

"She," I interrupted.

"What do you mean?" Rick answered.

"She," I repeated. "I'm telling you, your murderer is a she. And she knew both men up close and personal. I'm sure of it."

Rick slowly nodded his head but Tom almost imperceptibly shook his. Rick was at least doing me the courtesy of pretending to give my opinion some merit.

"Are you letting everyone go home?" I asked, trying to conceal my disbelief and disappointment at this turn of events.

"That's about all we can do," Rick said. "We have no legal

grounds to keep anyone here," he continued. "Tomorrow morning we'll tear down Meeting Room C and take all our files back downtown with us."

This time it was me who slowly nodded.

"Before we go," Tom spoke up, "have you been in contact with French?"

"No, not really," I said, figuring it wasn't a total lie since I hadn't even spoken to him.

Rick jumped on that. "What does 'Not really' mean?"

"I called Rains at Church Lane Depot on a hunch. French had been by to say hello but that was all Ted knew."

Now alert, they looked like two dogs responding to a high pitched whistle. I knew what they would do next. They would jump into their cruiser, put the lights on with no siren and race up Interstate 4 to shake down Ted for more information. I must call and give him a heads up that Laurel and Hardy were on their way. I was sorry to have drawn him into this, but that's the way it goes sometimes. And that's how taxpayers' money gets wasted.

Rick and Tom made their excuses and got up to leave. I walked them to the front door. *Adios, Don Quixote and Sancho Panza.*

"Jake! Jake and Lily! We need to talk," I called, as I re-entered the living room. They had disappeared into the den while the officers were visiting. They trotted back and we had a pow-wow.

"Jake, Lily, what do you say we break into Murder Central before they tear it down tomorrow morning? There might be some clues in their files to help solve this case. They haven't told me anything they know—I can feel it."

"Is this necessary?" Jake asked, looking to Lily for support.

"What else have we got? We'll never be able to access the police files any other way," I answered.

"Are you in, Lily?" I asked her.

"Does the pope wear a hat?" she asked me and continued,

"Are you sure you're up to this, though, Maya?" There was concern in Lily's voice.

"Don't you worry about me," I said, "This isn't even a flesh wound—I bet it's not as bad as getting a tattoo." I waved my slinged left arm.

"I'm not letting you two go alone so I guess I'm in, too," Jake said. "How do I let you get me wrapped up in these things?" He looked toward the heavens, shook his head and whispered, "Lord help me."

"Oh, baloney," I countered. "You guys love this stuff. How dull your little lives would be without me. Lock me in here and go home to change. See you later tonight."

Chapter 39

We decided to break into Meeting Room C around midnight. I asked Jake to do the pre-mission legwork. As a Sapphire employee, he was able to pop his head in and ask the police if they needed anything from room service or housekeeping. They declined, but he used the moment to find out that they were packing up for the night around 10. He reported that the guys were still in there, but the vibes were very low key.

At 11:00 p.m., Lily, Jake and I were gathered together in my house, dressed in black and wearing tennies. We sipped at the strong cups of tea I had brewed before they arrived.

"I take it you want us to be alert," Lily said, as she hoisted her cup and added, "Chin chin."

"That was the general idea," I answered.

"This tea is going to go right through us," Jake said.

"That's why we're gathered here at 11:00 p.m. Plenty of time to have a case of nerves and get it out of our systems, so to speak. Did you ever notice that this house has five restrooms?" I answered.

Lily changed the subject. "What do you think we'll find?"

"Probably some files we can copy. Let's pray that the notes they took in the interviews are still lying around. They must have created files on everyone they interviewed and what about

French? They may have some info on him that they're not sharing."

"You've probably had this same thought: even if they took great notes, would they know how to interpret them?" Jake asked.

"That, dear Jake," I said, "is why we must find those notes."

* * *

We walked through the reception area on the ballroom level. It was not a hot ticket at 11:55 p.m. We didn't need a smoke bomb in order to create a distraction while we jimmied the door open with a crowbar.

No, this operation was a lot more laid back than that. Jake used his master key and the three of us waltzed right into the darkened room. We had brought flashlights so we wouldn't have to put on the ceiling lights and call attention to ourselves if security strolled by. Once we were in, I took off the sweater I had tied around my waist and stuffed it into the crack under the door. We were free to roam, but I didn't want to hang around too long.

Eureka! We found the files right away, stacks of them, filled with yellow legal sheets covered in handwriting. I was doing a victory dance when Jake began waving his arms like a scarecrow gone wild.

What did he want? Was he joining me in my dance? He put a finger to his lips. Then I heard it, my heart pounding like a bomb that might explode in my chest, as I held my breath. We all doused our lights. Footsteps paused in front of the door. I felt light-headed. *No, I can't faint. I have to be strong.* Two men talked, rattled the doorknob, then moved on.

A minute later, Jake was the first to put on his flashlight. His pupils were enormous with fear. Lily was leaning against a desk with her face in her hands.

"That was too close for comfort," Jake said. "Maya, Lily, go, go, go, go! Let's each turn on a printer and make copies, then get the hell out of here before they come back."

It took forever for those sleepy old printers to fire up but, when they did, so did we. We copied everything, then made like hockey players and got the puck out of there.

Chapter 40

It was Thursday morning. Florida sunshine streamed through the French doors of my bedroom and onto the bed, where I sifted through the photocopied files.

"Are you decent?" Jake asked through the bedroom door.

"Sometimes I'm profane," I countered. "Come on in."

"Good morning, Maya," Jake said, as he elbowed his way in, carrying a tray with a teacup and fresh berries in a footed glass bowl.

"So, Jake, how is it we never got married?" I asked, thinking about how much I loved this man.

"Maya, Maya, Maya. Don't you remember we've agreed never to speak of that?" he said.

"Oh yeah, that's right. I'm missing the proper attachments. I remember now," I answered with a smile.

He set the tray down and told me he was leaving for work. He gave me strict instructions not to leave the house nor to open the front door. I agreed and Jake left, just as the phone began to jingle.

It was David Enderly. He wanted me to come to the hotel to meet him for lunch in a few hours.

"What's up, Dave?" I asked.

"I need your advice on something and I also want to tell you a few things. I'd rather not talk on the phone. Please meet me at La Croqueta."

"Okay," I said, hoping he'd have some insight on someone or something. I dialed Jake in his office. He said he would escort me to La Croqueta, our gourmet restaurant on the ballroom level.

That settled, I took my time looking through the files. I made separate stacks for each person interviewed and added notes of my own where applicable. There was a lot of reading but, in spite of that, I learned very little new.

I was disappointed that the police had not conducted thorough interviews with Alana and Mona, the two widows. Was this the Achilles tendon of southern gentlemen? I had no such weakness and became determined to speak to Alana and Mona myself.

When Jake came for me, he asked what I had found in the files.

"Next to nothing," I admitted.

"That's a disappointment," he said. "And to think, we nearly died of heart failure getting them."

"Yup," I said, discouraged.

"Did they have any news on French?" Jake asked in a hopeful tone.

"Nope," I said.

* * *

We entered the restaurant and Jake talked to the maitre d', Enzo Rossini. Soon we were following him to Enderly's table. Dave rose, shook hands with Jake, gave him the obligatory invitation to join us and Jake did the ritual, "No, no, I couldn't—I have too much work to do, but thank you," before he left.

"Hi Dave, what's up?"

"You're asking me?" he said, with a puzzled look in his eyes. "I invited you here to ask you the same thing. I was only hoping I could wheedle some information from you." He looked around like a cornered animal. "I am not up to this challenge, Maya. That's off the record, of course."

I nodded but didn't interrupt what seemed like it was going to be a good rant.

"First Torrey, then Vacaar are murdered, then you get shot. What in the hell is going on here? This is supposed to be a resort, a place where people come to relax and play with their families. How can we expect people to keep coming here, when people are dying and getting shot?" He spoke quietly, yet I could hear a thin edge of hysteria in his voice.

"I want to ask you something, Maya."

"Sure."

"Have you ever heard anything about Frankie Messina being connected to the mob?" Dave again looked around, as though he were being watched.

"Sounds corny, doesn't it?"

"I'm serious," he said.

"Okay, Dave, I'll be straight with you. Yes, talk like that does follow him around. He's always given me the creeps," I added.

"I knew it!" Dave said, with a note of satisfaction in his voice.

The waiter interrupted and took our orders, not that I expected to eat much. Dave's angst was contagious and this conversation was making me tense. Was that an itch I felt on my torso?

Just then, I saw Dave's wife, Margie, out of the corner of my eye. She walked up to our table and asked if she could join us. David said yes, then jumped up and kissed her cheek, pulling out a chair for her to be seated.

Margie enquired as to my wellbeing, clucking sympathetically and showing great interest in my bandaged arm. The waiter took her order and I asked her about her kids and school. She went on and on about them. Then, she told me about their summer sports programs and what good swimmers they were.

The more she talked, the more uncomfortable Dave looked. I

reckoned he had told her everything that had happened at the hotel. Now that she was sitting with us, he was afraid she would give something away that was supposed to be confidential.

Did it matter? Soon, with the police taking the files downtown, everything would be all over Orlando. She continued to babble, while we waited for our lunch to arrive.

La Croqueta served a shrimp scampi salad that approximated poetry. Tableside, the maitre d' prepared and then served me prawns with shiitake mushrooms on a bed of aioli-drizzled fiddleheads. The delicate aroma of herbs and seasonings happily distracted me from David's tension and Margie's ceaseless chatter.

Truth was, she was a little annoying. She was even more bright and bubbly than her normal perky self. Come to think of it, she had been nearly giddy every time I had run into her lately. For someone whose husband was working around the clock, she was far too happy. The obvious thought came to me—maybe she was glad that David was seldom home these days.

Was it my imagination or did her face light up while Enzo prepared my scampi? I wanted to warn her. I wanted to tell her about being a hotel wife, but I could no sooner do that than teach her Russian verb conjugations over coffee and dessert. Every hotel wife had to find out these things on her own.

She was either in it for the long haul, and learned to adjust to lots of alone time by building friendships with other hotel wives and filling her days with playing tennis or golf, getting manicures and pedicures and going to endless lunches with the gals, or she turned into a bitter little side show.

She could cultivate a public persona as the accessory to a high profile man by devoting herself to meaningful charities and fundraisers, improving her husband's and her own standing in the community, or she could ignore propriety and do her own thing, something she might later regret.

A good hotelier didn't notice his wife's loneliness. His hotel was his life, his work, his wife and his mistress, all rolled into one. A hotel could keep a man busy every day of his life, around the clock, and could provide a bed at night, too.

Every transfer from one property to another meant a fresh start from the ground up. Hotel wives paid their dues over and over again until their Honorary Lifetime Moving and Re-Locating cards lost their magnetic strips and had to be replaced. Still, it was a step up from being a suburban housewife.

The hotel life included hobnobbing with politicians, dignitaries, royalty, the rich, the famous, and the very rich and the very famous. Turn down service and mints on the pillows each night weren't bad, either, unless you fell asleep on them, drunk, like Philip Trotter once did. He woke up in the morning, looked in the mirror and began to scream. He thought his left ear had hemorrhaged and death by brain tumor was imminent.

I wanted to tell Margie about my own near-death hotel wife experience. I wanted to tell her about a Rooms Exec in Aruba, who had been attentive and solicitous while French worked himself into exhaustion, getting the first mega Sapphire Resort in the Caribbean off the ground. Mr. Rooms Exec was Johnny-on-the-spot and always at my side with tea, sympathy, Remos Fizzes and open-topped jeep rides along the empty highways that followed the coastline of the rocky, little island. While French worked twenty-four hours a day in the resort, this man gave nearly the same amount of time to working on me.

Johnnycakes was aboveboard and on the up and up until one evening that ended with a midnight ride in a classic, convertible XKE. My guard was down as we sat, watching the waves lap against the shore. I felt a tender kiss on the nape of my neck and it felt good. With a sick shiver, I realized I had to get back to French—now. I belonged with him and not this bottom-feeder.

I wanted to say to her, "Margie dear, I know how easy it is to feel flattered by someone's attention, when Mistress Hotel takes your man, wraps him in her velvety black-out drapes and fluffy down comforters, leaving you alone at home, night after night." But I knew she wouldn't hear me. She had to walk this road alone, make her own decisions.

These were my private thoughts at lunch as Margie's doe eyes followed Enzo around the restaurant. Enzo's interest in Margie, every time he visited our table, was also unmistakable. Dave was oblivious to the vibe. When the absurdity of the situation became too much for me, I looked the other way and right at a piece of Death by Chocolate, a signature Silver Pines torte.

Dave, Margie and I shared a slice of the hazelnut and truffle concoction with espressos on the side. Nobody's troubles, not Dave's, Margie's, Enzo's or even my own, were ever worth missing a good dessert.

Chapter 41

When lunch ended, I called Jake and he walked me back to the house. He checked each room, closet, bathtub and under each bed, then gave me a sweet little kiss on the forehead and locked me in. I said goodbye to him and was flooded with a wave of sadness.

Why were two Sapphire guys dead? Why was French still AWOL? Why was I here alone with my arm in a sling and my spirits in a slump? Why did Margie have to look so happy every time Enzo walked by? Why was David so blind to it?

I knew the answers. They had to do with hotels, ambition, sleazy men, neglected women, greed and personal grudges. Those were the biggies. Why then, could I still not put any meaningful clues together and find the murderer? I felt like a great big flop, a loser and a lonely one at that.

Normally, this would be a perfect time to throw myself a little pity party; I could feel my throat start to constrict and the tears welling, but the phone rang and ended all that. I cleared my throat and said, "Hello?" a few times to the beams in the ceiling before I picked up the phone for real. No use in sounding desperate for a call; it might ruin my image.

French! It was French! Could it be true?

"French, I can't believe it. Is it really you?"

He sounded unlike himself. His voice was muffled and it came from far away. "Maya, Maya, it's the man in the moon," he half-rumbled, half-spoke.

Why was he using this silly code? I knew it was him. "I hear you. Where are you?" I managed to blurt out but he spoke right over me.

"Meet me late tonight, early tomorrow, in the wee hours. The wee hours."

"Okay. Sure." I knew which wee hours he meant. All I needed was a place.

"Meet me where the egret spreads his white, feathered wings. Alone. Tell no one."

"Okay," I said, but he was already gone.

I got it. I knew he was keeping it brief, in case the line was tapped.

I was so excited, I wanted to scream out loud. I didn't dare. Who knew what else was bugged around the house? Instead, I locked myself in the bathroom, turned on the shower full blast and, with the water rushing like winter run-off from the top of Mt. McKinley, I laughed, yelled, whooped and hollered and did a little Maya dance of joy.

Chapter 42

I wanted to ask Alana some questions. The last few times I had seen her, bad things had happened to me afterwards. I called Lily to come with me, even though I knew Jake stood at the ready to escort me. No way was Alana going to be unguarded around Jake. She hardly knew him. Alana knew Lily from activities we had enjoyed together as corporate wives.

I called Alana and made a date to meet her at 9:00 p.m. in her suite. In the meantime, I had a lot to do. I wanted to go over the photocopied notes again. Maybe I'd missed something. I climbed on the bed and pored over them yet another time.

One might have thought I'd be too excited about seeing French to fall asleep. One might have thought my brain would be on overload, trying to find the solution to this vexing human puzzle. One might have thought those things, but one would have been wrong.

I had been running on nervous energy and too little sleep for too many days in a row so that now, I was out like a kitten. Was the Egyptian goddess Isis the guardian of kittens? If so, it was into her arms I fell.

I dreamed that I plowed a go-cart into my therapist's pet elephant, an elephant that had been in the family for years. The elephant exploded when I hit him and pieces of grey elephant hide flew into every corner of the room.

Just then, the house phone rang and my head nearly cracked in two. I was too out of it to pick up the phone. Plus, I was afraid it would be French, telling me he had changed his mind and wouldn't meet me later.

So, I didn't answer, but let it go to message. I wished I had not. Hitting an elephant in a dream was better than being hit with this, a man's disembodied voice, speaking in a monotone, "Maya, you are so God damned dumb. Keep your stupid nose out of this."

Sleep was out of the question now. Isis wouldn't be cradling me again any time soon.

Chapter 43

I was thrilled to see it was after five. Jake would soon be back from work, so I fired up ye olde tea kettle. I had fallen back asleep after all and gotten a few good solid hours of good shut eye. I would need them, as it turned out, but I didn't know that as I got out the tea cups and shortbread biscuits for Jake's and my little snack.

I leaned against the kitchen counter and took mental inventory, as I watched the blue flame flicker along the bottom edge of the kettle. I had one dead Sapphire president and one dead Sapphire regional veep. I had two mourning widows, or so it appeared, some cuckoo on the loose who liked to play with bullets, belts and pantyhose, a kidnapper, Monotone Man on my voice mail and a husband somewhere, who was slated to make a cameo appearance later tonight.

Who woulda thunk it? When we moved to Orlando three years ago, it was the sleepiest little mouse hole on earth. It just went to show how wrong a girl from L.A. could be. Weirdos were not limited to the streets of West Hollywood, after all.

The field of suspects was wide open. Either of the grieving widows could be a magician with pantyhose. Frankie Messina was a shady guy who would probably not let a little thing like murder stop him from getting ahead. He was tight with Philip

Trotter. Trotter might kill to ascend to the Sapphire throne. Once he was the man, he'd be handing out plum properties like poker chips. Those closest to him would benefit; they'd be able to pick the resort of their choice. He and Messina could be in cahoots.

So many people within the corporation stood to benefit by Red's death. Only one person benefitted from Vacaar's death. That would be Mona, but if my feminine intuition was right, she was innocent. She carried on enough, crying through her mascara, to be real. Something told me that she and her Albanian prince charming had been gaga about each other.

While waiting for Jake, I listened to Monotone Man's recorded message a few more times. There was something about the message, something familiar about the voice, something, something. What? What? My muddled mind tossed the clues around like Enzo would have tossed a Caesar salad.

The phone rang again. What would it be this time? Each time it rang, the red light flickered. I watched and scratched my tummy before picking up. The welts below my ribs were back with a vengeance.

"Maya, this is Mona." Her voice was sad, teary. "I'm so confused. Who would want to kill Vacaar? Who would want to kill Torrey? I need your help. Can I come see you tomorrow afternoon? I'm losing it. What do you say?"

"I say fine. Come by around 2:00 p.m. tomorrow, after lunch."

We rung off and I wondered why she had called me? We had known one another for years, but were never terribly close. Did she know something she wanted to share with me? She claimed to require my help and that was worrisome.

I needn't have worried too much. A lot more soufflé would be baked, rise and fall before 2:00 p.m. tomorrow.

Just then, Jake walked in. I couldn't wait to spring my mystery phone message on him for some feedback.

"Hi, Jake! Get over here," I gestured to him with enthusiasm.

"What happened to hello?" he asked.

"Hello! Now get over here," I said, continuing to gesture.

"Gee whiz, Maya, hold your horses. You're flapping your wings like a hen protecting her chicks. What could be so important?"

I played him the recording a few times. He made clucking sounds and tilted his head to one side, looking a lot like the RCA Victor dog.

"Sounds to me, crazy hen," he said, fluttering his wrists to mock me, "like you better get smart and solve this case pronto."

Chapter 44

Jake relaxed elsewhere in the house after tea and I went back to studying the files we had stolen. Lily arrived at 8:00 p.m., armed with salads and sandwiches from Tammy's.

"You don't expect me to eat now, do you really?" I asked her.

"Why not?" she said. "Look, Jake's interested. His nose is twitching already."

It was true. Men could eat any time, I guessed. I picked at a few green things with little enthusiasm. Lily and I prepared to walk together to Alana's suite. Jake was to drop us at her door, then disappear nearby and wait for us. I showed French's small hunting knife, tucked inside my waistband, to Lily.

"What in bloody hell?" she said. "What do you plan to do with that, gut a fish?"

"Oh, ha ha," I said. "I don't want to go there unarmed."

"You look foolish, Maya," Lily said. "Leave it in French's sock drawer. I've never seen a sinister side of Alana, but even if she had one, she'd be no match for us. Have you forgotten my black belt?"

"Why do you think you're going with me?" I asked. "Still, a black belt is no match for a bullet."

Lily scoffed, "And a knife is?"

I followed her orders, we locked the doors and started walking to the hotel. Sometimes, it felt like most of my life was spent walking between the house and the hotel. Sometimes, it felt like most of my life was spent making nice-nice with near strangers, and forcing myself to look interested in stuff that made me yawn. Sometimes, it felt like I was married to a phantom and, without my friends, my life would have been empty and meaningless.

I thought about my buddies, Jake and Lily, and how I loved them. We had enjoyed many adventures together over the years, both here and in Hollywood, London, and North Carolina. We'd get through this one, too. A modern day Three Musketeers, that was us.

Chapter 45

The interview with Alana did not go well. She was as closed up as a burger stand on the beach in January. Lily and I made chit chat and tried to get her to open up. She offered us drinks and we accepted.

She joined us and held her liquor. Being a cheap drunk myself, I was starting to feel woozy. I was little and lightweight. My blood alcohol level rose faster than hers or Lily's.

The only thing Alana did was sigh out loud every few seconds and twist her big fat diamond wedding ring around her finger. In all the time I had known her, I had never seen her do that before.

After about twenty minutes, she screwed up her courage and asked us, "You don't think someone made a mistake, do you?"

"How so?" I ventured.

"I mean, you don't think someone meant to shoot me and not you, do you, Maya?" she continued.

"How could that be?" I asked her, "You and I couldn't look more different. Who would mix up a petite brunette with a pedigreed blonde?"

"Someone angry, someone bitter," she answered. "What about someone who resents us both?"

"Is there such a person?" I asked and looked over at Lily. She shrugged her shoulders as if to say, "What a bunch of rot."

We sat there like three dummies, pondering that possibility. I began to feel uneasy and wished we could leave. Both Alana and I had a past with Sapphire Resorts but now, only one of us had a future.

It was impossible to avoid the obvious. "So, what will you do once you get back to Chicago?" Lily asked.

"I haven't the vaguest notion," Alana said. "I'll have to get Red into the ground, then there will be the obligatory face off with his adult children from his first marriage. That won't be pretty. They're going to want everything he left behind except me. I'm a big stumbling block to their getting wealthy as quickly as they'd like."

Another sigh and then she said, "Don't get me wrong, but I'm just not in the mood for company tonight. I have no new ideas that might shed light on this topic. I'm as clueless as you are, maybe more so. Let's all get a good night's sleep and call it a day." With that, she led us to the door, gave us each an air hug and kiss, and sent us on our way.

"What a bloody waste of time," Lily said to me as we walked away.

"You're not kidding," I agreed. I felt stupid for asking Jake and Lily to come along. Nothing had happened. What did I think would happen? Did I think Alana would cave and confess that she had always hated Red and Vacaar, too?

That had not been likely. Hearing about her adult stepchildren made me consider them in a new light. Could one of them be skulking around Orlando, trying to find a way to cash in on dear old Dad? I got the sense that Alana considered herself a target, and maybe she had a point. The possible culprit pool just got bigger and I was in the deep end, treading water.

Chapter 46

Jake, Lily and I were trudging back to my house, talking between us, when a large net fell over us. A net? What was this, Jungle Land Wild Animal Park? Men sprang from hiding places and surrounded us.

Even as the unreality of it hit me, we were falling over each other, groping at mesh, trying to get back on our feet and not succeeding. I had the weird sensation of being in a bad B movie. Nothing sophisticated about it. This stupid maneuver smacked of local yokel dumbasses. Who were they and where was the Orlando PD when the three musketeers needed them most?

It was a moonless night and this part of the path, between the hotel and my house, was shadowy, a perfect place to string a net between some tall palms. The three of us wriggled and struck out at our captors with a fierceness they did not expect. Between kicking, screaming and throwing blind punches, we were doing a decent job of dispatching these guys. They were buffoons, I could see that, all dressed in black with pantyhose over their heads, of all things. *How fitting,* I thought, with a grim sense of irony.

Somehow, we beat those guys. I managed to kick one of them in the shin, and I kneed another one in the groin, much to my satisfaction. Moans and grunts filled the air. I could hear Jake punching someone and Lily was spitting fire like a hell cat. The goons turned tail and ran almost as quickly as they had attacked us.

We untangled ourselves from the net and heard the sound of sneakered feet pounding over the bermed landscaping and in the direction of the parking lot. Then, we heard a car peel out. Whoever they were and whatever their goal, they were gone now and their bizarre little ambush had not worked.

Jake, Lily and I were all jabbering at the same time, checking each other out to make sure we were okay. I was unsteady on my feet and my nerves were shot. I felt as vulnerable as a blind man at the edge of the Grand Canyon. Once more, tears were springing to my eyes when Jake said, "Well, this is another fine mess you've gotten us into, Maya," in his best Oliver Hardy voice.

Lily started to giggle and Jake joined in. Before I knew it, I was laughing, too, and wiping away my tears at the same time. We were so upset, we had to laugh to keep from crumbling.

Jake gathered the net in his hands and dragged it along for closer inspection at a later time. He wanted to call the Orlando PD, but I wanted to keep it quiet. They had failed to protect me when they were in place. Who needed them now?

"Listen, Jake," I said, "I think it's a bad idea to call the police for many reasons, not the least of which is, I think this may have had something to do with these morons."

"What?" Jake said. I could feel his eyes flashing at me, despite the darkness. Lily echoed his incredulity.

"Yes, that's right. Wasn't there an adolescent whiff about this escapade? Face it—this was almost a joke."

"You're right about that," Lily piped up. "If they meant to give us a scare, they succeeded, but that still won't stop us, will it? We're unstoppable."

"You got that right, sister," Jake chimed in. "We scared them a lot more than they scared us. If we hadn't been tangled up in that net, I know I could have taken them singlehanded." He pounded on his chest with his free fist, à la Tarzan.

"Absolutely, dear Jake. Absolutely," I said. "Once again, you're my hero."

Chapter 47

I was one lucky duck! Several hours had passed and my two sidekicks were sprawled out in my family room on the cushy leather sofas in front of the TV. Jake had the net at his feet, as though it were a trophy. Lily was curled up on her side, with a throw pillow clutched to her chest. The excitement must have tuckered them out; they were down for the count. Of course, it helped that I had insisted we toast one another and our killer karate skills with a Jaegermeister or two. While they tossed theirs back, I dumped most of mine into the ficus planter next to my overstuffed chair.

I wasn't a big drinker and couldn't even down a whole shot at one time. Sipping and flinging, I was able to outlast them both and now I sneaked to my boudoir. I took a quick shower, put a fresh bandage on my shoulder, took two Tylenol and ditched the sling. I didn't need it. My arm was just a little sore.

I blew my hair dry and applied fresh make up. Everything had to be right. My heart pounded all the way to my ears as I dressed in the clothes I had selected earlier today for this secret meeting with French. It might seem silly to anyone else but I was wearing new, lacy, black underwear beneath my black, long sleeved top and jeans.

I was crazy with excitement and my stomach was doing cartwheels at the thought of seeing French again. Typical me, my brain function was beginning to recede and my animal cravings were kicking in.

Knowing him, he might be more business than pleasure, but I fully planned to insert some pleasure into the equation. Would he insert himself into me? No, not too likely. French was not a big one for public displays of affection and he didn't have a daring streak in him like his crazy spouse. No way would he risk being caught in a compromising position on hotel property, not even with his wife. French was a keep-it-in-the-bedroom-behind-locked-doors kind of guy. I should probably try some Jaeger shots on him sometime.

I slunk out the front door, quiet as a mime behind glass. I carried a tote with a pair of black sandals to change into but, on my feet, I wore a pair of rubber Wellies. There were several roundabout ways to get to the open air meeting space across the lake where French was waiting for me. They would take at least a half hour. If I took the kayak we kept tied to our deck, the trip would take five minutes from start to finish.

Part of me was hesitant and squeamish. The kayak could be filled with black racer snakes or even water moccasins. I hated those slithering buggers, but I was desperate to get to French and I was not about to traipse all over the property. The kayak was the way to go.

With my heart still racing and butterflies in my stomach, I made my way to the dark side of our deck. I had a tiny flashlight with me. No way was I getting into that kayak without checking it out first. If I actually found a water moc or a racer, I didn't know what I'd do. Trudge back to the house, put on a pair of rubber gloves and bring out some barbeque tongs, I guessed.

I looked in the kayak. *Phew! No snakes—thank You, God.* I untied it from the slip, pushed it through the muck and thought about our manmade lake. It wasn't super deep. Still, alligators often migrated to it from the nearby marshes. I had kayaked upon it dozens of times in the daytime, but never once at night. The thought of meeting one of our six foot, snaggle-toothed reptilian friends was terrifying. My mouth was dry and I trembled with nerves, but I jumped into the kayak anyway, and shoved off. It slid silently across the calm water. Nothing could stop me from taking the fastest way possible to seeing French, not even common sense.

I paddled along with eyes only for the opposite shore. I was so intent on meeting French that I didn't give the lake the attention it deserved and, in the pitch black night, I hit a bump. The kayak lurched and I, taken by surprise, overcorrected. The next thing I knew, I was submerged in the cold, murky water. Water filled my mouth and nostrils and I began to choke. Sputtering and coughing, I descended and the Wellies slid off my legs. My feet, now bare, sunk into the slimy, gooey mud on the bottom of the lake. Not a strong swimmer, panic hit me in the back of the neck like a two by four. I was going to drown.

I pushed against the bottom and felt the silt sucking at my ankles and toes, as I tried to release myself from its grip. The water felt as thick and heavy as split pea soup against my now-heavy clothing. I struggled against the weight of it and, just when I thought I could hold my breath no longer, I made it to the top and drew a long, gasping breath. Shivering and with my teeth chattering, I felt for and found the overturned kayak in the dark. I clung to its side and swam toward the opposite shore. I was hyperventilating. I was a filthy mess. No one but me could have been that clumsy except maybe Inspector Clouseau, and he wasn't real.

I breathed in long sharp gasps, and I was too shook up to cry. I was off-balance and I felt humiliated. Now I would look like a drowned rat, as I emerged from the water to meet French. It wouldn't exactly be Venus rising from the depths, fully formed, on the half shell.

Chapter 48

He had his back turned to me as I neared him, slosh-sloshing, at our meeting place.

"French—" I said, "it's me!" as tears welled in my eyes. I felt ugly, stupid and embarrassed in my wet clothing, dripping onto the wooden deck, with my hair hanging down in limp, soggy ropes. And I had wanted to look so special for him!

"Good God, Maya, you look a fright." He started right in on me, after he turned and took a few steps toward me, then stopped. "What the hell have you done?"

Before I could answer, "I did this all for you," he was laughing. French was not a man who laughed easily or often but, my appearance tickled him, and he didn't stop laughing for what seemed like a good three minutes. I stood there, at first happy that I had made him laugh, but then, he didn't stop. He was on a jag and, as he wiped tears of laughter from his eyes, I began to feel insulted and resentful.

"Look, you ungrateful bastard, this is what you get for disappearing on me for days on end," I spat at him, starting to work up a big head of steam.

"Oh please, Maya," he said. "If you could only see yourself, you'd understand." This time he doubled over with laughter, his hands on his knees. I said nothing, just glared.

A few seconds later, he pulled himself together, adding, "I'm just disappointed, that's all. I had it in my mind that I was going to hug and kiss you as soon as I saw you and not let you out of my arms for a full five minutes before we even started to argue, but you managed to surprise me, as always," he said.

"Well," I said, somewhat placated, "at least we had the same intentions."

"Sit down," he said, pulling out a wrought iron patio chair for me and one for himself. "I want you to know that the past six days have been hell for me, literal hell."

"Oh really?" I answered, in disbelief. "They've been a picnic on the grass for me."

"Ugh," he said. "Going for sarcasm, are we? Sarcasm is the defense of the weak. You taught me that, remember?"

"I *am* weak," I said. "I'm weak and I'm exhausted. It's been complete insanity here since Friday night. You have no idea since you haven't been around for any of it." I could feel hot dark clouds of resentment gathered in the back of my throat.

"Are we going to get into a competition now, Maya? Am I going to have to tell you each lousy thing that happened to me and then you're going to top that each time with one of your own tales of tragedy and drama? I have never known a woman as competitive as you," he frowned.

"Oh, never mind," I said, giving him a raspberry. "I'm sure you didn't come here to pick a fight with me."

"No, I didn't. I've been trying to track down some leads I got through Ted Rains. Someone left him a recorded message about Torrey's murder, saying he knew it was Alana and giving the reasons why. Then, he got a letter the next day, telling him I was involved and the sender claimed to have proof that could put me away forever."

"What?" I said. "That's ridiculous on both counts. What did you do then?"

"I tried to lay low and figure out who was behind this. It didn't help that the cops were crawling all over Church Lane, looking for me. I'm beginning to feel like a runaway slave on the underground railroad. Rains has passed me from one safe house to another from Maitland to Ocala to Longwood and back."

"Aw, honey," I said, my voice and my heart beginning to soften. "It hasn't been easy for you, has it? I had no idea."

"No, Maya, it has not. I'm about to turn myself in to the cops. I might be safer in their custody. I have the uneasy sense someone is watching my every move, just waiting to pounce when the time is right."

"No, French, no," I protested. "Please don't do that. I don't trust them. They're either inept or else something more disturbing is going on behind the scenes.

"Honey, keep flying under the radar for another day or two. I'm sure I can get this thing figured out. I've got Jake and Lily helping me. We're going to shake everyone down and gather clues until we find the killer." What would be the point in telling him about Luzi, that a bullet had nipped my shoulder or that Jake, Lily and I had round housed our way out of a net only a few hours ago, like something from a Three Stooges comedy?

"Maya, I hate to do this," he said, standing, "but I have to get out of here. I can't risk security or anyone else finding us here like this."

"I know," I said, getting up, with sadness in my voice. "This interview is over."

He grabbed me then and gave me a hefty, full-frontal hug. Not long enough to get all the juices flowing, but long enough to take me by surprise with a long, deep kiss that made me buckle in the knees.

He pulled away from my wet and shivering body, looked down at me and said, "Maya, sweetheart, you're beautiful. Wet, dirty, frightened, angry, it doesn't matter. You're a sight for sore eyes and I love you." He hugged me till I thought he might crush me. Then one more quick kiss and he disappeared into the night.

Chapter 49

I was still plenty wet but at least my spirits weren't as damp as they had been for the past week. Just one good kiss from French had made me feel alive and given me a new zest for finding the murderer. I was ready to roll.

I knew something was wrong the moment I tied up the kayak, so I edged back to the house with misgivings. The place was lit up like Christmas. I had noticed the lights go on while I paddled back toward home. It was sure to be one kind of trouble or another.

If it were Jake and Lily, they would have my head for sneaking out on them. If it were other people, they had to be bearing grim news. No bad guys would turn the rheostats to high in order to advertise themselves.

I looked through my front door and saw Rick Wells and Tom Koenig standing in my living room, with Jake and Lily seated in the oversized club chairs in front of them.

"To quote Yogi Berra, 'It's *deja vu* all over again,'" I said, as I entered. "Didn't I walk into this very same tableau 36 hours ago?"

"It's hardly the same scene," Rick said, squinting at me as though someone had just let in a skunk. "Have you been out for a swim in your clothes?"

"I felt like running through the sprinklers, so I did," I answered.

"Tell it to the judge, Maya. We're booking you and you're coming with us. We're asking you some questions at the station." Rick drew out my name so it sounded like someone had stepped on a cat's tail. "Linda Messina was just found, face down, at the far end of the lake. Someone shot her clean, at the base of her skull."

Jake and Lily looked at me with bug eyes.

"Oh my God," I said, a stab of horror hitting me in the solar plexus.

"Do you remember telling us, just a few days ago, that you didn't like her one bit and, if it were up to you, she'd be sleeping with the fishies?"

"That slipped my mind," I answered, though it was the first thing that had come to my mind, as soon as Rick mentioned Linda's murder.

"Is that a fact?" Rick said.

"I didn't mean it," I said. "I was just upset about that bullet whizzing past me. I had the sense that she or Frankie or one of their Mafioso type buddies was behind it. Why aren't you out, rounding up Frankie? He's a snake. He'd ax his own mother if he thought he might win a Cracker Jack ring for doing it."

Rick interrupted me. "We're on it, Maya. That's none of your concern."

"And what about Alana Torrey?" I asked. "I saw her having a little *tête a tête* with David Enderly and Linda Messina yesterday afternoon in the gift shop."

"We'll be running her in for questioning, too. Don't you worry your little head about that, sweetheart," Koenig added.

Sweetheart? I wanted to put him in his place but now was not the time. I zipped my lip.

Jake and Lily sat mute, looking like See No Evil and Hear No Evil. I asked Rick if I could at least put on some shoes. He nodded and asked Lily to get them from the closet for me.

Lily rushed to get the shoes. "While you're back there, Lily darlin'," Fatman Koenig shouted toward the master bedroom, "bring a bath towel with you, would ya, please? I don't want yer fancy friend, Mrs. French, drippin' water or leavin' mud all over our cruiser. We just had it detailed." I wanted to deck him.

Before I left with Rick and Tom, I turned to Jake. "Call Doug Reed for me and tell him to get me out of jail. His private number's on the rolodex in the den." Jake nodded.

Rick led the way. I followed him and Tom brought up the rear. That's where he belonged. I sort of thought of him as one great big rear.

Chapter 50

"If this were official police business, could you accommodate me?" I asked into the phone, sitting at my desk. From here, I could see the lake and the white winged bandshell on the far shore. A slight shudder passed through my body at the memory of being there in French's arms not eight hours ago.

Doug Reed had gotten me out of the clink first thing in the morning. Since Rick and Tom were coming to our property anyway, they gave me a ride. I had been with them more lately than with anyone else. Maybe we were going to be the new three musketeers.

I had slept a few hours, cleaned up and was sipping a strong, hot cup of tea while I made a call. Elevator music grated through the phone. I was on perma-hold. My welts were acting up. I scratched my tummy, as the Musak played.

I had to figure this sucker out before French caved and turned himself in. He was tired of running. He wasn't the fugitive type. He was the grown up boy scout type, a straight shooter. He didn't believe in hiding from anything or anyone. I knew, if he turned himself in, it was as good as saying, "Hey, look at me. I'm a murderer."

Rick and Tom were single minded. To them, it was either 1. Hubert French, 2. Maya French, or 3. some shady underground type who had killed Linda Messina. I kept telling them that I was innocent and that French was, too. He was at the right place at the right time last night to have killed Linda. They didn't know that, though, and I wasn't about to tell them.

I told them that Linda's death was not related to the other two, but they didn't believe me. That husband of hers had never been up to any good. He radiated phony—his suits too expensive, his jewelry too garish, his gifts to Linda over-the-top. He often bragged that his people came from Sicily. Trite as it sounded, he probably was connected to the mob.

I was certain of it—Linda's death had nothing to do with the others. Her death was unlike the other two, but it ran even deeper than that. I also had the sense there'd be another death soon, I just didn't know who would be getting their wind cut off this time.

The outline of a murderer was beginning to emerge from behind the left anterior cortex of my right-sided brain. Trouble was, I needed facts to back up my hunch. Rick and Tom would never listen to me, unless I could shower them with indisputable facts.

There was a knock at the front door. Keeping my promise to Jake to never open the door uppermost in my mind, I got up and peeked at the door. I saw a tall shadow. A shadow of a shapely woman, who was tossing her hair back over her shoulder. I stepped forward for more of a peek. It was Mona Luzi.

She was supposed to meet me at 2:00 p.m. What could she want here now? She was a suspect but my gut said that she was innocent.

"Come in, Mona," I said as I opened the front door wide. "Sit down and join me. I was just having a cup of tea. Give me one minute, though, I'm on a call in the other room." In my office, the phone was still playing Musak. I hung up and went back to the living room.

She was standing with her back to me, one long, cool drink of water. Ah, to be a leggy, Danish blonde with the face of an angel. What her life must be like, I could only imagine. *Doors must open for her every where she goes.* What was I thinking? Against Jake's strict orders, hadn't I just opened my door for her?

"So, what brings you here now?" I asked. "I thought we were getting together later?"

She turned quickly to face me. I had surprised her, snooping through our floor-to-ceiling bookcase. "I'm sorry, Maya. I took a chance you'd be in now. I couldn't wait. I'm so restless these days."

"That's understandable," I answered.

"Here, I want to give you something," Mona stretched out her hand. She gave me a little box, wrapped in pink tissue paper with a silver ribbon. I set it on the coffee table.

"Come, sit down," I said. "Do you like Golden Assam?"

"Oh sure, sure," she said, sounding distracted, as she folded herself into one of the living room club chairs. Her long legs in linen shorts stretched forever in front of her.

I watched her from the kitchen as I prepared the tea. She had a residual sadness about her, much like Alana, yet she was relaxed. She didn't give off the vibes of a strangler or a cold-blooded, pistol-wielding executioner. I walked in with her tea cup and sat down in the club chair beside her.

"Go ahead, Maya, open it," she prompted me. "I want to see if you like it."

For this very reason, I hated receiving gifts. I tried to cultivate neutral expressions, but people told me they could read my emotions on every feature of my face. Faking enthusiasm for things I didn't like was almost impossible.

No worries this time. I carefully opened the wrapping and pulled the lid off the little white box to reveal a sterling silver brooch. It was a stack of three teacups on a saucer. From behind the stack, a plump rabbit appeared with a goofy smile on his face. The cups were enameled in bright, happy colors and the rabbit was enameled white. His eyes were cabochon rubies.

"It's beautiful, Mona! Why ever did you think to give me this?" I asked with heartfelt enthusiasm.

"Haven't you heard? I make jewelry. Everyone at Sapphire knows how much you love tea, so I made it for you. I brought it from home and, with all the troubles, I almost forgot to give it to you. Do you like it?"

"Like it? I love it! My favorite book is *Alice in Wonderland*. You couldn't have made me a more perfect gift. I'll cherish it always."

Her face broke into a wide smile. "I was hoping you'd like it."

I gave her a quick hug and placed the box with the pin on the coffee table in front of us. It was hard to think of someone so sweet and talented as being capable of murder. Still, since she was here, I thought I should ask her a thing or two.

"Mona," I started, "I need to ask you a few things. Were you and Vacaar close with Red and Alana?"

"No, not especially. The guys worked together and we saw them at the usual Sapphire functions. Other than the occasional lunch with a bunch of Sapphire wives, Alana and I didn't get together much."

"Oh," I said, disappointed.

"It was Vacaar," she continued, "He was closer with Alana than I was. They shared a serious interest in golf and classic cars."

"Is that so?" I said. I hadn't known that. *Maybe Alana and Vacaar had become close, but not quite as close as Vaccar thought? Maybe Alana had used Vacaar to get rid of Redmund and then, when Vacaar had became a liability, she had found a way to get rid of him?*

"I know this is painful, Mona," I forged ahead. "Can you imagine who would have wanted to kill Vacaar?"

"I can't. I really can't. I think about it every waking moment of the day and night and I have plenty of those. It's not like I've slept very well since Vacaar—" and her voice broke. She looked away and put the cup to her lips, taking a shaky sip of her tea.

A nice display of grief. It almost seemed scripted. After a little more conversation, she got up to leave. I walked her to the door and thanked her again for the beautiful pin. We air hugged and she strode gracefully toward the gate, like the tanned, blonde, ex-super model that she was.

Chapter 51

The Sapphire corporate execs would only be here for another day and a half. My sense of inner frantic was mounting. I was applying calamine lotion by the bucket, but the fiery red welts on my midriff gave me no peace.

I paced back and forth on the travertine tiles in the entryway of my house, scratching myself as I walked. I didn't expect my guardian angel Jake for a while. As I paced, I talked out loud, summarizing the clues I had gathered. Had someone been watching me from outside, the men in white coats might have been called to take me away.

I had rung Alana earlier and invited her for a bite to eat at Papa's Place. I planned to ask her about everyone who was still breathing on my original suspect list.

I intended to talk with Frankie Messina, too, but how? That might require some finesse. Dave Enderly had phoned and told me that Frankie was locked in his suite, both distraught at Linda's death and also angry at Rick and Tom for shaking him down, as though he were Linda's murderer. What an ego.

Rick and Tom wanted to haul Frankie to jail downtown but Dave assured them that Frankie was fine in his suite and would stay on property. I'd figure out how to get an audience with him later. Right now, I made a reservation for two, overlooking the lake, at Papa's.

I changed into a melon colored silk and linen blend suit and slipped on some low-heeled sandals. Jake came back and escorted me to the restaurant. On the way, we ran into Lauren White. She had a black, leather portfolio tucked under one arm, and clippity-clopped on her dainty heels past the pool area toward the side entrance of the hotel lobby.

"Hi Lauren!" I greeted her. "Where are you going, at this time of day?"

"Oh, hi, Maya! I'm taking a report to David. He needs the numbers on Tuesday's shindigs," she told me, then looked down at the uneven flagstone path as she moved away.

"Keep your eyes open, my pretty," I said.

"Shut up, Maya! You're giving me the creeps!" She gave a fake shiver.

The walkway split into two; she went to the left, to the hotel, and Jake and I took the winding, uphill path on the right to Papa's. I was not going to spare Alana's feelings at Papa's Place. I had been ueber kind so far and handled her with jeweler's gloves but now I was going to look right into her lupine blue eyes and get serious with the questions. It wouldn't exactly be a drilling but it wouldn't be a cream puff tasting, either.

Later tonight, our disco, Orange 43, would be the site of the last evening event of the conference. I was going to get into Chloe Trotter's face, lovely as it was, to see what I could see. I hadn't focused much on Philip and Chloe, yet they might be the couple most inspired to create a new life for themselves as President and Mrs. Sapphire Resorts.

In the last eight hours, no new corpses had been found. Maybe Linda Messina was going to be the last person killed, but I had a hunch more trouble waited ahead.

Whoever killed Linda did so for a different reason than whoever killed Redmund and Vacaar. Yes, the method had been different, that would be obvious to a fifth grader. But more than that, her killing was blah and by the numbers. It lacked a certain *je ne sais quoi* that the first two had demonstrated.

Just as I turned the corner to Papa's Place, I tripped over a new sculpture. It was a goose with eight tiny goslings, all clustered around mama. They were sculpted of green jasper or marble or granite or whatever sculptors use to sculpt little creatures that end up in the corners of footpaths on resort properties. This sculpture was nearly invisible, nestled amongst the ivy and jasmine.

Good lord, who placed it there, where it can hardly be seen and why? The sculpture garden should have been renamed the obstacle course. More than once I had scuffed the toes of sandals, pumps and boots on wayward sculptures and I wasn't the only one. I had seen David Enderly almost take a flyer the other day. I had seen guests get tripped up, as well. To me, the sculptures were too big a liability in exchange for giving the hotel a little class. They provided guests with a handy reason to launch a law suit, which would finance their next vacation and then some.

Maybe I should contact *my* lawyer. But no, he was busy keeping French and me out of jail. I also reminded myself it was poor form to sue the hand that fed French and me, as I rubbed my sore toes.

One evening, French and I had been entertaining the Sultan of Barwani and two of his favorite wives at Papa's. As we left the restaurant together, I looked over at Hassa—he had asked me to call him by his first name—and blam! I landed right on my face. My toe had nudged the toe of a cast iron armadillo, newly placed at the edge of the path, and I dropped like a penny down a wishing well.

The Sultan rushed to help me back up, as did his veiled and concerned wives. French asked if I was all right, but he probably wanted to crawl behind the nearest sculpture—a large, wild boar in repose. None of Hassa's wives had tripped and fallen, only Maya.

I got the last laugh, though. Much to French's annoyance,

Hassa sent me fifty, long-stemmed, yellow roses the next morning for friendship and maybe for how my skirt had flown up to my waist as I fell. If he had not been full up at four wives, I'm sure I would have gotten an offer from him.

Today, the hostess at Papa's greeted me with the manufactured, fawning smile trained into all Sapphire resort employees and seated me at my table. As I waited for Alana, I looked around the room. It was humming like a well-tuned Porsche. Papa's was alive with the music of people's voices and their laughter, accompanied by the sounds of glasses, silverware and plates. Busy servers were running hither and yon. Sommeliers, with their little silver wine spoons dangling from chains on their velvet vests, were showing expensive bottles of wine to their grape-loving customers. Tantalizing aromas wafted in the air.

The hostess led an elderly, unkempt gent in wrinkled, baggy clothing to my table. I was about to protest when he sat down and, in a voice that I recognized, said, "Hi Maya! What do you think?"

I almost slid from my perch. For a moment, I could only stare. Flabbergasted, I said, "I think you're having an out of body experience. What, in the kingdom of heaven, are you doing in that get up?"

Chapter 52

"I'm scared to be me right now. I can't believe you're tooling around this property as though nothing unusual were going on," Alana said.

"I'm sorry. What did you just say?" I was too distracted by her get-up to pay attention to the words coming out of her mustachioed mouth.

"I said," she continued, with just a hint of exasperation, "I'm afraid to be me right now. I thought it might be smart to go underground for a little while. Jacko does this all the time."

"Jacko? Who's Jacko?" I asked, thinking Alana might have snapped her banana.

You know—*Jacko,*" she said, lowering her voice as she looked around the room, her blue eyes darting from under bushy, old man eyebrows.

"What? You mean Michael Jackson? Is that to whom you're referring?" Now I sounded a tad exasperated.

"Yes! That's exactly who I mean. You know Red, MJ and I have been friends for years."

"I do?" I said, stupefied by this unexpected information.

"Well, sure. We met through the Donald a few years ago at a charity affair in New York."

"Hey, I'm stuck out here in Wallyworld. What do I know?"

She continued. "I told Jacko I'm wigged out."

"How? When?" I asked.

"I called him on his private line. His secretary told me he was out here. What a coincidence, huh? He rented a horse farm in Ocala for a few days—brought some friends. You know he loves Disney, don't you?"

"Yes, I know he loves Disney. Everyone knows that. French has been trying to lure him onto our property since we opened, promising him everything but the moon on a sliver tray to entice him."

"Jacko got me this disguise. He had one of his people bring it over. He has several of these outfits. Variations on a theme. He always goes to Disney World dressed as an old man."

"Well, flip my frittata!" I said. "Not only is he not recognized, but he and his party get onto the rides first, using the wheelchair line." I was both disgusted and jealous.

French and I often kidded that we should provide a "Rent-a-Grandparent" service next to the shuttle bus entrance of the hotel. Elderly locals could be made available, for a fee, to escort our guests to Disney. They could then sit in wheelchairs, cut the long lines for rides, and see five times what the average visitor to Disney could see in an eight hour day.

It was a win-win idea; our guests would be happy and they would also be helping to boost the financial well-being of the local senior citizens. And now a do-it-yourselfer like Michael Jackson had figured this out on his own, the clever bastard. *Maybe all is not lost. Maybe we can carry a line of Old Man Costumes at the gift shop.*

"Okay, on to another topic," I said, regaining my mental footing, "Why didn't you tell me you and Linda Messina were thicker than thieves?"

"Linda and I go back a long way. I thought you knew that, Maya. When we were young, we worked together in Chicago before I met Red and she met Frankie."

"What are you saying?"

"I'm saying I was a bunny and Linda was the room manager."

"What?" I said, "You and Linda worked for Hugh Hefner?"

"That's right. She didn't seem the type, did she? But, she was never a bunny," she added quickly, "Always a manager."

"I see," I said, seeing nothing.

"I don't like to think back on those days," Alana said, after a pause. "Linda was aware that I didn't like people knowing I had once worked for Hef. She and I kept one another's secrets when we graduated to a bigger, more social world."

"Well, shoot, Alana. I never knew you were a bunny. You kept each other's secrets well. Does French know?"

"It's possible," she said and shrugged.

I was sitting across from a hunched old man in baggy, well-worn pants, a tweed jacket, a white shirt with some genteel stains that bleach had not removed. He was wearing shabby, brown shoes, wire rimmed glasses and a little felt hat that made him look like Giopetto. And this was a former Playboy bunny. *I am living in an insane asylum,* I thought as I unconsciously shook my head. *I have to strike out and make a new life for myself when this is over, I just have to.*

"All righty, then," I said, motioning for her to go on.

"Linda seemed to think she had seen something suspicious the other day," Alana continued. "I actually thought she might have killed Red, so I played along."

"Oh?" I said.

"Yes, Linda was my 'friend,' but she was always envious of me. I pretended not to notice. She also had a big crush on Red, and I know he took advantage of her feelings from time to time."

"Ugh," my lip curled.

"Yes, Maya. I'm sure you feel disgusted. You don't understand my world," she huffed, with a self-righteous shrug of her withered, old geezer, shoulders.

"You're right, I don't," I answered, *and I am ever so grate-*

ful.

"I thought maybe Linda killed Red and Vacaar until she herself was shot. You know what else?" she asked.

Part of me didn't want to know what else, but I gave her a look that said, "Go on."

"Linda had lost her charm for Red. He was on to the next little tart. Every time Vacaar's East Bloc back was turned, Red was all over Mona like a bear on honey," she said.

Oh, brother, I thought, *these people are far too complicated,* but aloud I said, "Oh, how interesting." After a slight pause, I added, "So you and Linda were on the outs."

"Yes and no. History and hurt make strange bedfellows, or at least peculiar friends. It turns out misery really does love company. We needed the support that only we could give to one another."

She stopped, then added, "I don't expect you to get it, Maya, not really, being married to French, who's such a ____" and she made the sign of a square in the air with her forefingers.

"Oh, trust me, honey, I get it. We all weave such tangled webs. Some of them are rectangular, trapezoidal or even square." No one was going to beat me at geometric comparisons, or make me feel less worldly, even if my husband did happen to be faithful. Or at least he appeared to be. Who really knew these days, when women were delivering themselves to men like pizzas?

"Look at this, Alana," I said to her, changing the subject, "what do you make of it?" I showed her a chart I had penciled on the back of the note I received that had told me to run. For one thing, I wanted to see if she recognized the stationery.

She squinted through her old man glasses, looking just like an addled, half-blind codger. "What's this supposed to tell me?" she asked, looking puzzled.

"It's supposed to tell when each victim was killed and whom I suspect."

"This is nothing but conjecture. So what if I was Red's wife?

So what if Linda was a special friend, and Red was overly chummy with Mona? I told you all that myself. I felt sorry when Vaccar was killed."

"Really, why?" I asked.

"He was a good guy, always attentive, ever the gentleman. He made me feel like a woman, yet he never went too far. Besides, we both loved classic cars. And, he was one hell of a golfer. He taught me a lot about swinging a club."

I bet—if that's what you call it these days.

"Yup," I said, "old Vaccar was almost a pro, all right."

She picked at her now cold food, dabbed at her mustache with her napkin and claimed she was full. She got up to leave and I stood, as well. Unexpectedly, she reached out, gave me a hearty hug and whispered in my ear, "You be careful, Maya French. Who knew you could be such a sweet friend? You mean a lot to me."

What was I supposed to do with that? I sat back down, my feathers simultaneously ruffled and smoothed. As I watched her shuffle out, I got the check, added a tip and signed it to French's account.

Chapter 53

My meeting with Alana drained me, and I almost broke my neck on a turtle sculpture on my way out of Papa's. I sat in the lobby, examining the scuff on my sandal and rubbing my toes again. I needed a moment to relax before I attempted a visit with Frankie Messina.

Relax. How did a person do that with the weight of three murders and a missing husband on her shoulders? It wasn't all on me, of course, but it *felt* like it was. Whatever top-notch police work Rick Wells and Tom Koenig were doing, it was artfully hidden from my view. They could have clued me in, but they were not that kind. I got the feeling they didn't much care about Maya French and might even be happy to see her land in the Silver Pines corpse pile.

I had to call on Frankie Messina to give him my condolences and to hear what he had to say about Linda's death. He had a motive to kill his wife, I now knew. Macho guys like him didn't take well to being cuckolded. Heck, he might have killed Torrey, too. His high up friends in bad places might have helped him on both counts. They knew how to get jobs like this done.

I was near the lobby bar, once again. The jazz riffs from the trio and the scent of tropical flowers and sun tan oil filled the air. It would have been a swell place to relax, had I not felt so jumpy. My waist was itching. I tried to maintain a lady-like demeanor and not scratch.

Instead, I focused on my navel with an old meditation technique. Breathe in, breathe out. On the exhale, let go. On the inhale, let God. It worked for a while, then it became: on the inhale, where's French? on the exhale, what now?

I got up and called Messina from a house phone to announce my arrival. No answer. It went straight into voice mail. He probably had the phone off the hook.

I called little Pam, French's secretary, and asked her if she had the info I had requested? She swore she was on it, working as hard as she could. I told her to dig deep, call whomever was necessary, and tell them it was a rush job. This couldn't wait much longer.

I had the hotel operator give me an outside line. I called the Walgreen's where the pantyhose on French's desk had been purchased. I asked for the manager, an older woman who had been pleasant to me on the first go-round. Instead, I got a manager on duty, some guy with a local drawl, who seemed to resent not only working the evening shift, but also me, for asking him to actually do something. His league was probably bowling tonight at Kissimmee Lanes and he was stuck at work. He put me on hold long enough to hang up on me.

Hah! He couldn't get rid of me that easy. I called back. He told me to hold on again—his boss's papers were in a messy mound on her desk and he couldn't find what I needed. I requested that he, this time, not put the phone on hold and lay it on the desk, until he could get back to me. It worked.

A few minutes later, with a martyred sigh, he told me he had the register tape. The pantyhose had been purchased eight days ago, three pairs, in the middle of the day. Even though he was a pill, he had come through for me. I was thanking him for his trouble, when he hung up on me, mid-sentence. Some people had lousy attitudes. Bad attitudes in Central Florida were no worse than bad attitudes in Southern California, they only sounded different—slower and more drawn out.

I tried to reach Messina one more time. No dice. I wished I had a pair of dice. I was almost ready to toss them. The dots on each die were starting to add up.

I gave up on seeing Messina just now and headed to Jake's office. "Hi, you!" I said, as I stuck my head in his door. "Is this a good time?"

"Oh sure, Maya. I was just thinking about you. I ordered something from room service. You can share it with me before I walk you back home."

"Thanks," I said, sitting in a club chair in front of his desk, "but I'm not hungry. Just had a bite with Alana and my stomach is unsettled."

"Here," he said, reaching in his pocket and handing me a roll of something. "Have a Rolaid. Let it roll around in your stomach and aid you."

"Why can't it roll around the resort and aid me in finding the murderers?" I asked.

"You can give it a try, Maya," he said, "but I doubt it will roll too far." He leaned back in his chair, and admonished me. "Why can't you leave this to the police, Maya? Just let it go."

"No, Jake. It's not that simple. I must figure this out. I have to," I said. Just then, a young man wearing a tuxedo rolled in a serving cart, and on it were a burger, chips and a cherry Coke.

"Will there be anything else, sir," he asked, batting his big, brown, velvety eyes at Jake.

I looked away, taking an interest in my manicure. Jake signed for the food and the server left. Jake looked at me and grinned, while he patted the left side of his chest with his right hand and whispered, "Be still, my heart."

"Oh gee," I said, rolling my eyes. "Is that all you ever think about?"

"No," Jake said, "sometimes I think about what people look like naked." He paused. "I also think about you, Maya, and how you're making yourself crazy over this. Do you mind?" he asked and turned toward his meal.

"No, go right ahead," I said. "Bon appetit."

"Thanks," he replied, biting into his big, juicy burger with all the fixings, "Are you sure you don't want to join me?"

"Really, Jake, no. It smells delicious but I couldn't." I twirled my chair left and right. Between bites, Jake spoke of a thousand things, just not the murders. I knew he was trying to keep my mind off French. It worked. I didn't think of him for the eight minutes I watched Jake scarf his burger, fries and Coke like a famished teenager on weed.

After he finished his meal, Jake slid open one of his desk drawers and pulled out a flat box that looked like it housed foreign chocolates.

"Here," he said, "take one. I know you're not going to turn down chocolates filled with cognac, no matter what shape your stomach is in. Besides, these things cure upset stomachs."

"I've heard that," I answered, as I reached for one and popped it in my mouth.

"Here, take another," he said. "One for the road."

I didn't resist. There wasn't one situation in life that couldn't be improved by good chocolate. If it was good enough for the ancient Mayans, it was good enough for the present day Maya.

Finally, Jake locked his office and, arm in arm, we walked through the sculpture garden, to my little house on the lake. I wasn't going toe to toe with that armadillo, turtle or mama goose again alone, not when I had a big, hunky guy to steer me out of danger.

Chapter 54

Jake deposited me back in my house, secured the perimeter and then went back to work. I knew I should get back to work, too, on solving the murders. I couldn't do it. I couldn't face them right now. I needed a break from all that crap before the remaining circuitry in my brain fried completely.

I had to occupy myself with something else for a little while. But what? The murders, French's disappearance, reappearance and re-disappearance consumed every ounce of my gray matter. I could feel one of my tension headaches coming on, starting as blurred vision in my right eye. I took two Tylenol and stretched out on the living room sofa for a few minutes.

I never did fall asleep or stop thinking about the murders. I was restless, I was agitated, I was spinning my wheels and burning rubber. I picked up the phone and dialed Lily.

"Lily, help!" I cried into the phone. "I'm going nuts. N-u-t-s, nuts."

"Oh dear!" she said, her voice warm and sympathetic. "What can I do to help?"

"Come visit me, Lily," I requested, "I know I should be working on all the clues I've gathered but I can't seem to face one more moment of any of it right now. It's all running together in my head and it looks like a Jackson Pollock painting in there."

"Speaking of painting, I was just finishing up an oil. Let me clean up and I'll be right over."

"Thank you, sweetie. I can't wait," I said. "Don't be surprised if I fall all over you in gratitude when you arrive."

I breathed a sigh of relief. Lily would distract me. She was a dear and, without her, my life in Orlando would have been one-sided and dull. She was my buddy and always up for an adventure when she wasn't tending to her cutting garden or working on ceramics, oils or mosaics in her studio.

Sometimes, she let me come play in the studio with her. She had formal training, talent and buckets of patience for my playing at art. I had a kid's curiosity about creating stuff. She let me feel safe while I set about botching portraits, or firing misshapen blobs of clay that I thought were vases. When I laughed at the hopeless junk I produced, she laughed with me but never at me.

She and William lived in a rambling, brick, Grand Floridian home, leased for them by the Norwegian owners of Silver Pines. Its two story, screened-in patio faced the eighteenth hole of the Bay Hill golf course. Each year, for the Bay Hill Classic, their home was the place to be.

Part of what I so liked about Lily was that she lived large, yet she didn't care one whit about the outer trappings of success. William was a former executive for American Cola. They had socialized with everyone on Atlanta's social register for years, before being transferred to Bangkok, then London and, eventually, Rome. When William retired early from Amco, he carved out a nice deal for himself and Lily with the Norwegian Pension Fund and was enjoying a second successful career.

The doorbell rang. I peeked and saw Lily standing at the front door, a baseball cap on her head and a large canvas leaning against her hip.

I opened the door. "Hi, Lily, thanks for coming." We hugged.

"Hi, Duckie. I could hear the desperation in your voice. Wild murderers couldn't keep me away." She placed the canvas against a wall, its blank side facing out.

"Please, don't mention the M word, okay?" I asked her. "I'm murdered out at the moment."

"I bet. Any luck discovering the identity of the mystery—?" she asked, smiling, and made a choking motion with her hands.

"No! Not saying the word 'murderer' and making a choking sign instead is still alluding to murder. Let's talk about something else, okay?"

"Okay," she agreed and added, "Here, I made a painting for you. Be careful, it's still wet." She turned the canvas to face me.

Against a velvety, plum colored background, there hung an empty noose made of tan pantyhose, the reinforced toes dangling from one side. It looked a little like used condoms.

"Lovely," I said, after I inspected it closely. "Just lovely. Doesn't remind me of murder at all. I'm going to hang it over the fireplace."

I propped it against the mantel, stood back and looked at it. I snickered. My reaction made her laugh. That's what she'd been going for anyway, with her gallows humor. It didn't take much to amuse us, really. We were easy.

I brewed us a strong pot of English Teatime and we played cribbage in the den. Sitting there, nibbling madeleines and drinking tea while we poked pegs into a board, made life feel almost normal.

"So, Maya, you seem a little better now," Lily said, after a while.

"Better than when you got here, yes," I said.

"So, what accounts for the change, dearie?"

"You came right over. You made me laugh. I don't feel alone anymore. Plus, sitting here relaxing with you, a few puzzle pieces fell into place. I have an idea who the killer is but I need a bit more time to get the details straight," I answered.

She left me to my thoughts while she dunked a madeleine, then ate it. My thoughts were flitting around like fireflies in a large, glass jar. They kept alighting on the notion of someone wanting prestige and social stature with a big helping of jealousy, lust and greed on the side. The more I tried to concentrate on who did what, the more the fireflies zigged and zagged. No pattern yet, no neon light flashing the answer in my brain, but I was getting close, I could feel it.

I'd have to mentally discuss this with French. Shortly after he had first been taken away in handcuffs, I started an ongoing inner dialogue with him. Some might have called it guided visualization. Some might have called it wishful thinking. Some might have described it as water on the brain. To me, it was a lifesaver. If I couldn't talk with French in person, talking with him in my head was the next best thing.

Lily and I watched part of "Dial M for Murder" on VHS. It was easy to buy evil deeds on celluloid. How had real life become so murderous?

A while later, Lily, affecting a Southern accent, said, "It's been fun but I gotta run. I have to rustle up some grub for my man."

"Sure," I said. "You better go."

"Jake will be here soon, won't he?" she asked.

"Yup," I answered. "He's due back any minute. I'll be okay. Give my love to William."

I set a new kettle of water on to boil and, like clockwork, a few minutes later, Jake walked in the front door. We had our tea. He snarfed up the leftover madeleines. We talked a little and then it was time to get ready for the farewell Sapphire event of the conference at Orange 43. We cleared the dishes and split up to change into our party duds.

The party had a 70s theme and French and I had bought vintage costumes weeks ago. It was easy for me; all I needed was a clingy, spaghetti-strapped, knee-length polyester dress with a slit up one side, dancing shoes, pouffy hair and heavy eye makeup. Jake came out of his wing of the house in French's costume: a three-piece, white polyester, bell bottomed suit, black shirt, gold chain, platform boots and a blond afro wig.

French couldn't have worn it better himself.

Going to a disco was the last thing I would have chosen to do, but this event had been planned for over a year. The Sapphire Manager of 1985 would be announced tonight. The prize was a $50,000 bonus plus a trip around the world, all expenses paid.

It made sense to have the final Sapphire event at the disco. Dancing was fun, upbeat, exhilarating. It was a vacation sport enjoyed by most people at hotels and resorts. People who wouldn't lift an ankle to scratch a mosquito bite at home, found the will to get up and boogie at a hopping hotel nightclub. Nothing said good times like laser lights, a fog machine and a sparkling disco ball hanging from the center of a mirrored ceiling.

Jake and I walked to the hotel along the lake in the moist night air, past where Linda Messina's body had been dumped. The entrance to the disco was fifty feet away. As we approached the unmarked, industrial, steel door to Orange 43, we could feel the bass thumping and throbbing from inside.

"Man, you know how I hate noisy nightclubs," Jake said. "The things I do for you, Maya."

"Yes, my love," I answered, "and I'm grateful. You know that."

He pulled two bright yellow, squishy earplugs out of his vest pocket and stuffed one into each ear.

"If you need my attention, Maya, you're going to have to tap me on the shoulder."

I nodded and gave him the thumbs up. Might as well start the sign language now. The host greeted us and took us to a table in the back. The place wasn't full yet but people were trickling in.

I saw a lot of familiar Sapphire faces. Some were missing but would arrive later. Some were missing for good. I didn't want to sit around when the music was so inviting. The toga-clad waitress took our drink order. I took Jake's hand and led him to the dance floor. My thoughts were always more fluid while I was in motion.

As I danced, I thought about women and what motivates them. It's said that men seek admiration while women seek love. It's said that women love money, therefore, they love men with money. I knew there was plenty of moola swirling around the world of Sapphire Resorts.

Most people seemed happy enough to climb the corporate ladder the usual way—slow, steady progress to the top, where the elusive brass ring dangled from the highest atrium ceiling.

Some people didn't want to trudge up the rungs one at a time. Some people wanted to float to the top like Peter Pan, rigged to a hidden belt by monofilament, and snatch that ring on a fly-by. You could never tell who was a Peter Pan, who was a Wendy, who was as innocent as Little Red Riding Hood and who was a wolf dressed in a hotel manager's clothing.

As I grooved and twirled, my thoughts became clearer. I felt like I was on the cusp of cracking this case, as corny as it sounded, when someone bumped my left hip.

"Hey!" I said, annoyed, but it was only little Pam laughing and pointing at me, so I broke into a smile.

"Gotcha!" she said.

"Did you bring a purse?" she asked me.

I had no idea what she was saying. She had to repeat it a few times over the pulsing beat. I finally understood and nodded my head. She pulled out some papers she had tucked in one of her pockets and handed them to me.

I didn't want to risk leaving them in my purse at our table, so I folded and tucked them between the cups of my bra. Thank heavens for assorted underthings, where you could always hide a lipstick, a few bucks, or, as it turned out, some papers. Before pantyhose, I used to put all my necessities in the top of my nylons. Ah, pantyhose! I loved them but at least one Sapphire guy I knew didn't look good in them.

At the end of the set, I excused myself from Jake to freshen up. As I applied new lip gloss at the mirror of the ladies room, I saw Pam walk up behind me. I could almost hear her.

"Maya, join us tomorrow for supper. We're having a few friends. It'll be very casual," she shouted in my ear.

"That's sweet, Pam, but I can't. I already told Dave and Margie that I'd get Jake to take me to their place tomorrow evening for barbecue. They invited a few strays and I guess I'm one of them," I answered.

The conference was over for most of the managers after tomorrow's buffet breakfast. For some, it had ended earlier. Usually, the guests left with a tote bag filled with goodies and souvenirs from the host property. This time, a few would be leaving with body bags. Not the sort of keepsake one imagined when planning a visit so close to the Happiest Place on Earth.

Just as Pam and I exited the restroom, Lauren White came breezing in. Lauren's cheeks were flushed, her eyes bright. Had it been anybody else, I would have suspected she had just snorted a line of coke. But no, not Lauren.

There were only a few other things that could make a woman glow like that—things a little more old-fashioned and a little more wholesome than extract of coca plant. They usually centered around love, lust or a good strong flirtation.

As I left the bathroom, I wondered where the hell my mind had been? The truth had probably been in front of my distracted eyes the entire time, but I was so focused on French and guests dying to get out of the conference, that I had missed it entirely. As I reflected on how dense I could be, I tripped over someone's foot. It belonged to David Enderly.

Chapter 55

Funny. I had been overheated just a few minutes ago but now, leaving the crowded area between the restrooms and the dance floor, a chill ran up my spine. I murmured my apologies to David for flying across his foot and made my way back to the table. Jake was gone, dancing with some girl or flirting with some guy on the wait staff, no doubt. I grabbed my purse, looked around to say goodbye and tell Jake where I was going, but he was nowhere to be found.

I walked through the rear exit to the elevators and called Frankie Messina from a house phone one more time. Still no answer. I pushed the "up" button. I had a sick feeling in my stomach that went nicely with my chill. *We all had our problems.* At least, I wasn't a murderer but I did know where to find one if I was ever in a pinch.

I got into the elevator and pushed my master key card into the slit that allowed entry to the VIP penthouse floors. No matter how upset Frankie was about Linda, it wasn't like him to miss a party. He was a political animal, after all. Left to his own devices, he would be very visible at the final function of a manager's conference. It would be his last chance to glad hand and kiss some higher-up ass. *He should carry a little stepladder around with him for just that purpose.* So why had he not been at the dance?

I wondered about guys like Frankie. From what rocks did they crawl out under? Did they have parents or were they raised by wolves?

How had he ever found a wonderful woman like Linda to marry him? Born to a wealthy Chinese silk manufacturer and his emigrée, aristocrat, Russian wife, Linda didn't need Frankie's position nor money. Who knew what made two people love each other?

As I rode up in the elevator, a little voice in my head whispered that maybe I should not be rushing to Frankie's suite. Did I need to be the first at the scene of yet another crime? It had been a luxury to have Rick and Tom off my back for a day.

At the last moment, I pressed the button for the floor below VIP. It had become a popular spot for our guests to stroll, almost like the promenade deck of a cruise liner. From that floor, they could face the lobby far below and see everything that was going on. Planters with draping cascades of bougainvillea and grape ivy were set at the top of clear, plexiglass balcony rails.

I exited the elevator but looking down at the lobby set off my vertigo, so I kept my head up. I looked nonchalant as I mingled with the stream of guests. I walked first in one direction, then in the other, considering my next move.

Maybe I would get up to Frankie's suite and the police would be camped out by the doors. If so, I would feel foolish and just slip away. Maybe the hall would be deserted, and I could knock on the door of his suite and he would answer. I didn't want to be intrusive, yet I did. What should I do?

I went up to his floor. No one posted in the hall. His floor was quiet. Too quiet? I knocked on his door and waited, picking the cuticle on my left thumb.

Nothing. I knocked again, this time harder. I put my ear to the door. *I do have a master key. What's it for if not for opening doors that otherwise remained locked?*

I said a little prayer, put the key in the slot and swiftly pulled it out. There was an almost imperceptible "click" and the door opened on its own, just a crack. *Open, sesame.*

I tippy-toed onto the black granite floors of the entry hall. This suite was a lot like the Munch suite, without the Munch on the living room wall. The Munch suite was also without the original Munch on its wall. The real Munch resided in a large vault on the basement level of the First National Bank of Orlando. Only French and I and our bank officer knew that. There was a fake Munch in the suite, but no one, not even the Norwegian owners who had given us the painting at the grand opening, noticed the difference.

"Frankie," I called. "Franki-e-e-e-e!"

No Frankie. I slid back out the way I had come. I grabbed a house phone in the hall and had the operator page David Enderly, so that he could investigate Frankie's suite with me. Dave didn't respond. If he was still at Orange 43, he probably couldn't hear a page or even feel a vibration, since the whole place was vibrating.

I went back to the lobby level. From there, I walked down the grand staircase to La Croqueta. I made a bee line for the bar and ordered a shot of Myers's dark run. *When in doubt, Myers's settles the nerves.*

I asked the bartender, a black-haired young fox with hazel eyes ringed in dark lashes, to give me a house phone. I rang Frankie's suite one more time. No answer. I hailed Pretty Boy over and asked for a second Myers's. Very unlike me but I was imbibing some liquid courage, just like the big boys. Three more gulps and I signed for my bar bill.

I went back to Frankie's suite, took a deep breath, and knocked. When no one answered, I had David paged again. This time, he answered and I asked him to come up. He was reluctant, as the party was still in full swing. I could hear the music and revelry in the background as we talked.

"Please, David, get up here. I need some back up."

"Let it go," he answered. "Let's call OPD if you're concerned."

"I'll wait for you at the elevators," I said.

He hesitated, then said, "I'll be right there. I'll bring Margie and, if I run into Jake, I'll bring him, too."

"Great," I said. *It'll be a happy fizzy party.*

"Deal," David said and then he hung up.

I waited. And waited. And waited some more. No David. No Margie. No Jake. Pacing back and forth in front of the bank of mirrored elevators, I caught my own reflection. I looked haggard, tense. The past week was taking its toll on me and it showed.

If no one else cares, why do I? Then I remembered. They weren't as motivated as I. I was ready to put this nightmare to bed so that I could, once again, share mine with the man I loved.

Chapter 56

I was antsy as hell and a call from nature came that would not be ignored. Nerves! I turned on my heel, and walked to Frankie's suite. This time, I didn't bother to knock or shout. I let myself in with my master key, turned right and entered the powder room. I held my breath as I switched on the light.

No surprises. This was good. I took care of business, then left the bathroom to look around the suite. It was bathed in dim light. I took some tentative steps into the living room. I looked in the dining room, and saw turn-down treats; a bottle of milk on ice in a silver bowl and a big plate of snickerdoodles.

Further left, I poked my head into the kitchen. Nothing. Everything was in order and jazzy elevator music played softly over the sound system. A dirge from Albinoni would have been more suitable.

Something about the scene was weird, staged. I was used to the artificiality of hotel life, but this was a different kind of fake that made the palms of my hands clammy. Even the two Myers's were doing nothing to calm me.

I called out, "Frankie?" No answer. I tried again.

Did I hear something upstairs, a mumbled gurgling? Maybe he was ill. Maybe he was prostate with grief. Maybe he was drunk. Maybe he needed help.

As a little girl, I hadn't aspired to be a nurse or even a wife or mom. The thought of finding Frankie upstairs, drowning in his tears or his own vomit did not appeal. Still, if I was the only one here, it looked like the job fell on me. Damn that David! Why wasn't he up here yet?

I walked up the stairs, groped for the light switch on the bedroom wall and, as I did, I tripped over something. It wasn't a marble turtle or a cast iron armadillo. It felt heavy and human.

Dread blanketed me as I flipped the switch. It was, as I had expected, Frankie Messina, face up on the floor. I had never seen him wear an ascot. Maybe he hadn't, either. This one didn't match his outfit and it was tied too high and tight around his neck.

* * *

"—and that's the way I found him," I said to Wells. He, Tom and I were together again, this time in Messina's suite. It was happening so often, I should probably start planning what songs we'd play on our reunion tour.

"Well, I'll be headed back to the lobby," I said, edging my way toward the stairs, since the guys seemed preoccupied with Frankie's corpse.

"Like hell you will, Mrs. French," said Rick and motioned to Tom to block my path. "Pardon my language, ma'am," he added, still a Southern gentleman to the core.

"You'll be staying right here, close to us," Tom, the refrigerator with the wide-legged stance, added. "Matter of fact, when I sneeze, you're gonna wipe your nose—that's how close we'll be."

"Charming image," I said, more to myself than anyone else in the room, dead or alive, and sat down on an occasional chair in the corner.

"You know what, Mrs. French? I may have been lookin' for love in all the wrong places," Rick said. "French has been AWOL all along but you've made lots of cameo appearances. I almost don't care anymore if or when he shows up. You're turning into a much greater person of interest to me. What do you say, Tom?" Rick said.

"I say we keep our eyes on her," Tom said.

The usual group of people arrived, ready to do the usual stuff—take photographs, dust for prints, scoop up hair samples and, in general, turn the place inside out. Rick and Tom flanked me as we rode the elevator down together. They had paged David and told him to wait in his office for us.

* * *

David sat behind his desk, looking pale. Margie sat in one corner with Jake next to her and I stood next to Rick.

This was the glummest gathering of living people, ever. Glum and awkward. Rick was, at first, conversational, trying to make this seem more like a casual meeting than an inquiry. It didn't work. David, Margie and Jake gave him clipped answers.

"Don't all shout out at once," Rick finally said. He turned to Tom and asked him to take Margie and Jake out of the room. He wanted to interview David with me present.

"Now, David," Rick said, "tell me again what you did earlier this evening?"

"I made the rounds of the hotel, like I always do. I was in constant radio contact with some of our staff, making sure everything was right at Orange 43 for the grande finale party of the conference." Dave looked edgy. Little beads of sweat were beginning to show near his hairline.

"Why are you so uncomfortable, David? What haven't you told us yet?"

Dave shifted in his chair. He cleared his throat.

"I saw Mr. French earlier tonight."

"What?" Rick and I said at the same time.

"I feel bad mentioning it, but I know I have to." He looked at me, his eyes apologetic, then continued, "After making my rounds, I saw him standing near the lake where Linda was found."

Unbelievable. I was stunned. It couldn't be true. If French

had been back, why had he not come to see me? Didn't he love me? Had the situation been reversed, I would have never come so close and not somehow snuck in to see him. It would have been my top priority.

I didn't hear the rest of what David said, I was so hurt and insulted. Me, me, me. I could only think of me. I felt kicked in the gut and it was only a tiny kernel of pride that kept me from letting the tears fall as they wished. Instead, I choked them back and tried to concentrate on matters at hand.

I tuned back in, just in time to hear David say that French had seemed out of it, and said a few things that didn't make sense, like "I see you there," and "I have to finish this thing."

"What did you make of that?" Rick asked him.

"I didn't know what to make of it. I asked him what I should do about running this place. I asked him when he would be back for good—was he back for good?"

"And?" Wells interrupted. "What did he say?"

"He waved me away, turned and walked through the foliage and the pines toward the gravel road the fire department uses."

"Why didn't you tell Mrs. French that you saw her husband?" Wells kept at him, then looked at me, "Did you know any of this, Mrs. French?"

I shook my head. I felt disgusted by the lot of them. They were all morons. My mouth was dry as a wad of cotton and I thought I might be sick.

Why are you standing here, talking to David, when the powers of OPD might be better used searching the grounds for one or more murderers that I'm sure as hell aren't French? I shot a few death rays from my eyes at Wells and Koenig.

"I was in a state of shock," said David, leaning forward. "I wanted to tell Maya when I saw her later at the party, but there was too much noise, and there were too many people. Then, she disappeared," he said, leaning back in his chair, looking relieved that he had told his story.

Chapter 57

It was Sunday after lunch. Jake had the day off and we were playing gin together in the den, while he, every few minutes, cast an eye at the TV. The water skiing championships at Cypress Gardens were being broadcast on one of our local stations. Water skiing was big business in Florida, hence the frequent, splashy coverage. The producers of the show switched things up by showing old black-and-white footage of human pyramids on skis, something people had been doing at Cypress Gardens since God Himself was a boy on skis.

I had a hard time getting Jake to play gin with me. He taught me the game during the summer we Eurailed through eleven countries in six weeks. By the time we hit Zurich, I was beating him with monotonous regularity at his own game and, by Vienna, he was done. It took me years to get him back into play mode.

We were half way through our third game when the phone rang. It was Wells. "Guess what I've got?" he asked, sounding vicious.

"I don't know. Let me think—a persistent rash that proves embarrassing at intimate moments?"

"Woah! Aren't we feeling sassy today?" he answered. "Well, that's about to change."

I didn't like his tone.

"Okay, sorry. You set yourself up for that one. I couldn't resist," I said. "I'm serious now, what have you got?"

"I've got someone very near and dear right here next to me," he gloated. "Actually, he's near to me now, but I don't find him very dear."

"Stop fooling around. Who do you mean?" I asked, feeling the hair rise on the back of my neck.

"I mean your better half, your beloved husband, French. He turned himself in about an hour ago."

"What?" I said, nonplussed. "You've got to be pulling my leg. You are, aren't you?"

"I most certainly am not," he answered. He called to his partner in the background, "Tom, am I pulling Mrs. French's leg?" There was a far-off, "No, you're not."

"My husband's confused. There's been some misunderstanding," I said, not wanting to believe French would do such a thing. It made no sense and it made him look guilty.

Rick didn't have much more to say. *Just spreading good cheer, huh?* We hung up after he reminded me that French would need a good lawyer, not some hack like Doug Reed, if he hoped to get away with less than four counts of first degree murder.

That was the end of Jake's and my game. I gathered the cards in a pile, as my spirits dropped below the posts supporting my house. I didn't do this much, and I never did it in public, but Jake wasn't public. I crumpled into the corner of the brown leather sofa and fell apart. I put my hands to my face and cried. Jake sat next to me for the first few minutes, handing me tissues, until I blew through all of them. He went to the linen closet, brought out a new box and set it next to me.

Of all the insane things French had put me through over the last ten years, this one was the top prize winner. I tried to be a good wife, I really did. I believed in him, I supported him emotionally, I performed like a trained poodle at corporate events and business soirées. I was tireless and he was wussing out—without discussing it with me first? It was exactly what I had told him not to do. It reminded me that he had been here on Friday night and not even tried to contact me, which upset me all over again.

Jake asked if I was okay.

"Not really."

"I'm getting you some Tylenol and a big bottle of Perrier," he said. "You're going to need both."

"Thanks," I managed to squeeze out, between sobs. "I can't believe this. I can't take much more of this."

"I know, sweetie," Jake said, full of sympathy, "You've been such a tough cookie. This was the drop of water that made the bucket overflow."

"I was so glad all the Sapphire people were gone," I cried. "I thought things would return to normal now, while Rick and Tom sifted through their findings and put their case together."

"That's how it seemed," Jake said, empathizing with me. He would have made a great therapist.

"I feel whipped. I've been blindsided. Put a fork in me, I'm done," I said. I felt flattened by a steamroller.

I looked up and took Jake's hand. "Sweets, I need to be alone for a little while. I need to cry myself out over this. You understand, don't you?"

"Not really, Maya. I'd think you'd want me to stay here to give you moral support," he said, protesting.

"I'm sorry, Jake. It's a girl thing, I guess. Come back in an hour or two. I'll be better then."

Grumbling, he said he'd go over to the hotel, hang out at the sports bar for a while and then come back, if I could handle that. I nodded and sent him on his way.

I had been reining in my emotions for a long time. We were back at square one and worse. Make it square zero. If French had turned himself in, a new nightmare was about to begin.

I gave in to my feelings and continued to cry until I couldn't

186 ~ Marta Chausée

cry any more. After almost an hour, I was exhausted and drained of all fluids. My sinuses above my brows and under my eye sockets felt like they might implode. I drank the bottled water Jake had brought me and I took the two Tylenol. I grabbed some ice for my forehead and lay down on the sofa, whimpering softly to myself and whichever palmetto bugs and wood spiders might be listening from what I hoped was afar.

I must have dozed off. For one tiny moment, I thought it had all been a bad dream. But no, it was real. My forehead was throbbing and I was parched. When they had worries, some people liked the noise and the hurries of downtown, but not me. I got up, my head pulsing, and wobbled into the kitchen for my universal cure. I knew I needed a big pot of freshly brewed, hot tea. If nothing else, I could hang my head over it and breathe in the steamy vapor.

Now that I was cried out, I felt lonely. I wished Jake would hurry back. *Women are impossible. No wonder you prefer men.*

With the tea kettle gurgling and showing signs of life, I splashed myself with cold water and brushed my teeth. My eyes felt like little puffer fish on my face. I refused to look at myself in the mirror. It would be too depressing.

Once the tea was steeping, I reached in the freezer and pulled out a frozen torte. There was always a stash of desserts in our freezer, created by our pastry chef, for VIPs, industry execs or the stray hotel wife or personal friend, who might stop by unannounced.

My mother often wondered how I could live in Grand Central station, as she called my life, with people popping in and out of my home at all hours. *This is how I do it, Mama. I'm always prepared. I'm a good Girl Scout.*

It wasn't just the goodies in the freezer. Open up the doors of the larder and you would find hotel sized containers of fancy mixed nuts, pretzels, trail mix and Red Vines. One shelf housed industrial-sized boxes of instant coffee, assorted tea bags and crates of bottled mineral waters. The wines, ports, sherries, cognacs, aperitifs and after-dinner drinks took up another entire shelf. Myself, I didn't care too much about alcohol but plenty of hotel types had their snouts in the bottle.

Our house was like a self-contained mini-hotel. If there were ever a collapse of the fabric of American society or a natural disaster, I'd be up to my widow's peak in food, tea, coffee, drinks and plastic water bottles. I had enough supplies to feed every person in the state of Florida for one entire year.

Chapter 58

The jackhammering in my head was abating and I was sitting down with a cup of green tea, when the phone rang. It was Lily. God bless Lily! She of the perfect timing.

"Want to come join me, Lily?" I asked. "I've got some news, I just brewed tea and I'm thawing something with a pistachio colored shell."

"Are you talking Swedish princess cake?" she asked, her voice happy. "I'll be right there."

When Lily arrived, she looked at my face but, like the good friend she was, said nothing. I gave her a general outline of Rick's and my earlier conversation, while we drank our tea and each enjoyed a slice of cake.

When we finished, we tidied up the kitchen and the house felt small. "Come on," I said, "Let's walk the nature trail around the lake." I left a note for Jake and off we went.

After a few minutes of walking and no talking, Lily started gently, "Maya, what are you going to do? Do you have an idea about an attorney? William might know some good people."

"French didn't do it," I said. "He won't need an attorney."

She was quiet a moment, probably thinking denial was not just a river in Egypt, and tried again, "But just in case, Maya—you have to start thinking of these things."

"No, I don't. You can't make me," I answered and gave the wood chips under our feet a stubborn kick.

"Ooh," she said to herself, as if something hurt.

After a moment, I asked, "Weren't you the one who told me it was impossible for French to kill anyone?"

"That was before he was conveniently without an alibi every time someone took a ride on a gurney to the coroner's office."

"Oh, come on, Lily. You know he's innocent," I said, annoyance creeping into my vocal cords.

"I do not," she said, now taking her life into her hands.

I said nothing. What was the point of arguing with her? She had her opinion and I had mine. Hers was based on what seemed to be facts. Mine was based on feelings, observations and experience. My bias toward French wasn't blinding me to the truth, was it?

Some flimsy shreds of knowledge, hanging in tatters from the mast of a tall ship, were bobbing above the horizon of my brain. I could pretty much see a face, feel an energy, get a sense of who was to blame for all this death. It was ugly. Morally bankrupt and spiritually ugly. I just couldn't stitch all those tattered strips together into a whole. Not yet. But I was close.

Poor Lily! She was trying to be realistic and helpful. I softened my responses and we fell into discussing my options. Eventually, we were talked out and walked along together in silence, as friends will, each deep in her own thoughts.

I thought back to Alana Torrey and her ridiculous yet effective disguise as an old man. Were there any celebs that she and Redmund hadn't known? What a life they had had together. Now, she'd be hoofing it alone. Or would she? As soon as word got out that she was widowed, there would be a long string of suiters camped outside her front door.

I hadn't had much interaction with Margie Enderly lately. She looked spooked and strange in David's office. Who wouldn't look spooked in a situation like that? She was a simple country girl, who was probably out of her depth in the hotel industry on the easiest of days and these weren't easy days.

And Lauren. She was still doing her job, being Miss PR, trying to make the Manager's conference seem like the big success it had not been. I thought about Mona Luzi, the dead Messinas and French's assistant, little Pam, with her shock of red hair and eyes as green as the hills of Cork.

Then I thought of French. It still stung when I thought of him, that idiot. How could he have not come to see me if he was here on Friday night? Maybe his elevator didn't go to the top floor anymore. Why else would he turn himself in?

Possession was nine tenths of the law and Rick and Tom had possession of French. Maybe he'd been bitten by a Lyme diseased tick at one safe house or another and it had affected his brain. I tried not to think about it.

I looked out over the lake. The sun was hitting it just right. If I blurred my vision, the light, dancing on the water, looked like sparkling crystals of sugar. Dancing. Dancing. Something about the dancing.

Lily was lagging behind me a few steps because she stopped to inspect a lizard, sunning himself on the path. He was missing his tail. I had grown up in lizard country and had held more than a few disconnected lizard tails in my hand as a child. They no longer impressed me, but I still enjoyed the feel of a little lizard in my palm. Their bellies were so soft and smooth, their little hearts beat so fast.

Lizards. No tails. Fast heartbeats. Dancing. Dancing. My thoughts darted and bobbed, as I squinted at the lake when, all at once, I had it. I had it! I stopped dead in my tracks as the coins dropped in my head. Lily, paying no attention, bumped right into me, which brought us both up short.

She mumbled apologies and I told her not to worry about it. I knew who the murderer was, but I wasn't about to spill the *frijoles*. Talk too much, act too quickly and you were likely to come up with only a lizard tail in your hand.

Chapter 59

From my kitchen window, I watched little Pam almost skipping down my garden path, her shiny red curls bouncing in the Florida sun. Over her left arm was a basket full of mail. I opened the front door before she could ring the bell.

"Hi Pam!" I said.

"Hi, Maya! Mail call." She unloaded the basket. "Postcard from Dave and Margie," she said. "I hope you don't mind, I snuck a peek. They're at the Lodge."

"No problem, thanks," I said. She left and bounced back toward the hotel. I looked at the card.

On the front of it was a nice shot of some old fart in waders, holding up a big fat marlin or whatever swam around the waters at the Sapphire Sporting Lodge on Islamorada. Why anyone would leave steaming central Florida, and I didn't mean that in the sexual sense, for the even steamier Florida Keys was a riddle to me, but that's what Dave and Margie had done. The back of the card stated they were coming back tomorrow night, and wanted a ride home from the airport. Odd, since they could have had livery from the hotel pick them up but, okay, if that's what they wanted.

There was also a note in the mail from Alana, inviting me to her cottage in Carmel, when the dust was settled. Earlier in the morning, Lily had come by and we played three sets of tennis. One of French's old buddies from Atlanta called. He was performing on violin in Orlando in a few days and wanted to take us to dinner.

"We might have to take a rain check on that one," I said.

"Why? I hope nothing is wrong?" he asked.

"No," I said. "French is on a business trip." Why should I tell Paolo everything? I didn't want to spread the word all the way to Atlanta. The word was already all over Orlando. I avoided my usual rounds at the bank, the grocery store, the cafés and other shops I used to frequent. I couldn't take the looks people were giving me.

Jake called and wanted me to meet him for fish and chips at the twenty-four hour restaurant near the pool for lunch. Mona Luzi called to say she was sorry about French. Her call knocked me out. As far as she knew, French might have killed her husband and *she* was calling *me* to show support? She was either saintly empathic or she didn't miss her Albanian stallion that much, after all.

My natural inclination was to isolate when I felt low. Contact and invitations from all these people were sweet, but were they lifting my spirits? No. I still wanted to stay in bed with the covers over my head until the world went away.

With French in jail, my life was the pits. Until everything was put right, I was existing, but only going through the motions. Things may have looked okay from the outside, but, on the inside, I was as raw as a banquet-sized portion of carpaccio.

Chapter 60

The following evening, Jake and I were at Orlando International Airport. We took the people mover to the terminal and were waiting at the gate, as happy tourists piled out of the plane. So many, in fact, that I began to think Dave and Margie had missed their flight. At last, I saw them clear the gangway.

They were talking and giggling, their heads so close together that they looked like an ad for Doublemint gum. We greeted them and they recounted with enthusiasm what a wonderful weekend they had enjoyed and why it had seemed like being newlyweds again.

We walked through Parking Lot B and made pleasant small talk as we left the airport. Jake and I sat in the front, with Margie and Dave behind us. Cruising westward on SR-528, we were soon headed north on Interstate 4. We exited westbound on Sand Lake Road and then turned north on Apopka-Vineland Road. As we drove, it was pine forests, an occasional clearing for a housing development, then more pine forests. Alligators lay in the culverts on either side of the roads and I could see their beady little agate eyes in the beams of our headlights, shining atop the water like marbles.

We took Sixth Avenue and turned right onto Main Street, Windermere. Windermere was a small town with its own chain of lakes, making it a desirable homestead for boating and water ski enthusiasts. Jake's condo was in Windermere, as was Dave and Margie's home.

Windermere reminded me of Main Street, USA, at Disney. It was old-fashioned and picture postcard perfect. I liked to go to the post office there. It had two mail slots in its lobby. One read, "Windermere." The other read, "Everywhere Else," as if Windermere were the center of the world.

As we made our way up Main Street, I knew Dave and Margie were expecting us to turn left on Third Street to get to their home on Pine. Instead, I asked Jake to pull the car into the parking lot of the First Baptist Church.

Jake looked puzzled but didn't say a word. Dave leaned forward in his seat, fidgety, and looked around.

"Why are we pulling off here?" he asked. Did he sound paranoid or was that my imagination?

"I thought we might have a little chat," I said.

"A chat? About what?" he asked.

Margie came to life. "What's going on?" she said, her voice concerned.

"Nothing. It's about the murders. I thought you might like to know what I was able to find out while you were gone."

"Okay," they said in unison. Margie looked relieved but David looked tense.

I turned to face them. "Dave, all along I reckoned that the murderer was either Alana or Mona. They each had strong motives and they were the closest to Redmund and Vacaar. They behaved strangely all along—Alana too calm and collected for a grieving widow. The same thing could be said of Mona, who remained more sequestered, but imagine this—last week, she brought me a little silver brooch she had made for me. I found that noteworthy. Who thinks of bringing gifts to a person when her husband has just been murdered—and in her own Chanel suit and new shoes yet?"

"They were at the top of my mental list, too," David answered and Margie nodded, her brown, rabbit eyes vacant yet scared.

"No matter how I looked at it, Luzi's death didn't make much sense. It wasn't a power move to gain the presidency of Sapphire, because, technically, Philip Trotter would have been the next in line," I said.

"That's true," Dave said.

"Then I found out, by accident, at the ladies' 'color' day, that Philip and Chloe Trotter were sitting on a big surprise that wouldn't be announced until July 1. He had been hand-picked by the Weinsteins to run their new airlines acquisition, Brennair."

Dave looked bitter. He had been passed over, but who did he think he was? He wasn't ready for a job like that.

On a hunch, I asked, "That didn't feel good, did it, Dave?"

"You're damned right." He raised his voice in answer to my question. "I should have gotten that job. Me. Dave Enderly. I deserved it."

"Calm down, honey," Margie said. "You'll get the next big promotion."

The sound of her soft voice calmed him.

I waited a moment for him to settle, then continued, "After that, I considered Frankie Messina. He stood to gain a lot, career-wise, with both Torrey and Luzi out of the way. Even though Brett Fitzpatrick was technically next in line for the presidency, he was too old and too much of a party boy to want the hassle. Life was good for Fitz right where he was. He would have happily handed the company over to Frankie and played second fiddle."

Jake and David both nodded in agreement.

"So, Frankie was my man," I went on, "but I couldn't get the goods on him. I saw you, Alana and Linda talking in the gift shop one day and wondered about that. When Linda and I went to the little girls' room at Papa's, she said she was worried about Frankie. She was vague. I didn't question her, but I had the sense it had to do with his outside life. His connections with the mob were always rumored."

"I know," Margie piped up out of nowhere, "That man scared me and I always tried to stay away from him."

"Me, too," I said. "When Linda was found dead, murdered in the way she was, I couldn't believe it. I mean, what were the chances that an unrelated murder would happen on our property? But looked at logically, it made sense. What a great time to sneak in a murder and not get caught. It looked like a typical hit—a gangland style execution. No bizarre clothing items were wrapped around Linda's beautiful, cultured neck."

"I thought about that, too. I figured Frankie had ticked off someone and this was his punishment," David replied. "Who knows what trouble he got into with his *paisans*."

"Exactly!" I said. "When he turned up dead a short while later, I have to confess, I wasn't exactly surprised."

Everyone nodded thoughtfully.

Looking at David, I said, "Dave, when we met at Luzi's, I noticed your suit looked limp and your hair was kinked and frizzy, as if you'd been in a steam bath. My hair does that, too, even if I only stand too near a steaming tea kettle for a few minutes. It made me think back to Luzi's death. I realized you had been in Luzi's bathroom before I got to the suite."

I turned to Margie, "This is going to hurt. I want you to hang in until I've finished."

Like a mouse face to face with a cat, she fixed me with a frightened stare. "Okay, Maya."

"But Dave," I said, turning back to him, "what kept going through my mind was how quickly you were at the scene of most of the murders and how often you had to meet with Lauren White."

David looked down and said nothing.

"Why I was blind to this so long, I don't know," I said. "I kept running into Lauren here, there and everywhere. She was her darling self, all high heels and short skirts, silky blond hair and dimpled smiles. Every time I asked her where she was going, she said she was bringing a report to you or conferring with you about something that I eventually realized was not very important.

"It was in Orange 43 that I had the ah-ha moment. I saw you lean into her when her back was to you. Margie stood to your left, but you leaned toward Lauren and you smelled her hair.

"That would have been enough, but what you did next was the real clincher. You inhaled and closed your eyes, lifting your head as you savored the scent. No man smells a girl's hair like that unless he's a goner for her."

He was silent, staring at the dashboard, a strange sheen in his eyes. His lips turned down in a frown.

"It wasn't much fun to play second fiddle to French and, on a larger stage, to people like Luzi, Messina, Fitzpatrick and even Torrey himself. For a guy like you with big ambitions, it had to be rough, especially when a woman as desirable as Lauren caught your eye.

"Lauren was innocent. She didn't know she was driving you to murder, Dave. She was being herself—young and high-spirited—when she flirted with you in her come-hither-yet-don't-touch-me, Southern belle way. Sure, she was flattered and even titillated by your attentions, but she's a good girl. She'd never consider taking up with a married man. However, a married man might look at her, want her and think of ways to rise to the top and take her with him."

Dave muttered and looked down at something only he could see.

I continued, "You framed French and then planted the pantyhose box and receipt in his office. It got French out of the way while you were killing people, and you got to be the big man on campus, all the while pretending you were insecure and needy. I bought right into it and did everything I could to reassure you."

It was getting stuffy in the car. I opened my window. Then I added, "Luzi knew something was up. He wanted to tell me what he knew but, somehow, you got wind of it and invited yourself before I got there. That was the end of him, poor guy." I hung my right arm out the window, waving my hand to someone unseen outside the car.

Dave, who had gone quiet, snarled like an enraged Rottweiler, and screamed, "You stinking little bitch!" as he lunged at me from the back seat, something nylon stretched between his hands.

It all happened so fast. He wrapped the pantyhose around my throat and pulled it tight, while I tugged frantically, trying to loosen it, unable to breath. David tightened the hose around his fists, increasing his choke hold. Jake erupted across the seat and, in one smooth motion, smashed David's face with a forceful left hook. I heard the bones in David's nose crunch, and blood splattered onto me, as he flew backwards against the rear seat. I heard a scream that rocked the car, though I don't think anyone noticed. It was mine.

Jake was pummeling David when Margie let out her own eardrum-shattering scream, tore open the left passenger door, and ran from the car. She careened and stumbled through the parking lot, screeching and squealing the whole while, like a pig at slaughter. Her man was a murderer; fists and blood were flying. On some level, she must have realized she was next on David's hit list. It was all too much for her.

Within seconds, six squad cars, with their lights flashing and sirens wailing, pulled into the parking lot and surrounded our car. Rick and his men ran toward us with their guns drawn. Rick threw open the right rear passenger door and yanked David out by his hair, dragging him onto the asphalt and smashing his neck against the ground with his boot. In moments, twelve Magnums were pointed at his bloody face.

I had spoken to Rick late Sunday night. When the post card from Dave and Margie arrived, Rick and I hatched a plan. Jake and I would pick up the two lovebirds and bring them to the

Baptist Church parking lot in Windermere. Rick, Tom and their men would be in place, waiting for us, hidden amongst the pines that surrounded the lot, with their engines idling and their lights turned off, ready to jump in when I gave them the signal.

Chapter 61

"Ma'am, do you realize your purse is open?" our twenty-something, bikini-clad waitress asked me, in a high-pitched, childlike, nasal voice.

"Gosh, no. I hadn't realized that, thanks," I smiled, twisting to close my bag, but French reached over and zipped it for me.

"Thank you, sweet thing," I said to him, leaning in and giving him a kiss on the neck, under his ear. He gave me a squeeze and smiled. French was his old self and more. It was day three of our getaway at the Sapphire Crystal Shores Resort in Key West, one of our favorite hideaways. I had laughed at Margie and Dave for going to Islamorada after the conference, and, here I was with my honey, on the southernmost key of all. The irony was not lost on me.

We were cuddled up on the beach in a loveseat under an umbrella, enjoying our view of the turquoise blue Gulf of Mexico. He sipped his Harvey Wallbanger and I nudged my thick and frosty Frangelico smoothie through a pink plastic straw. It was our turn to relax, soak in the late afternoon sun, suck up drinks with little paper umbrellas and coo at each other like newlyweds.

"I just can't believe it was Dave. I feel so stupid for not realizing it was my right hand man all along," French said.

"Don't feel bad, honey," I said to him. "You were too close to him to see it."

"How did you put it all together?" he said.

"Mostly, Lauren gave him away and she didn't even know. I ran into her wherever I was in the hotel. Her heels were always clicking smartly and she had some report or other that David had requested," I answered.

"After a while, it occurred to me that no one needed that many reports, no matter how green he might be or how insecure about running the hotel without you," I said. "Plus, he was sniffing her hair like a goon."

"You mean like this?" French asked, burying his nose in my hair and breathing in with a sigh of satisfaction.

"Yeah, kinda like that but not so passionate, more weenie-like," I giggled. "While you were gone, David kept in close touch with me. His insecurities were over the top. That was odd for a guy who's been in the hotel biz since he left college. Let's face it, David's not a kid and this is not his first property. It started to seem like the old saying, keep your friends close, keep your enemies closer.

"In the beginning, dummy me was feeding him all sorts of information. Once I got an inkling that he was the guilty party, I started feeding him lies, not that it helped much," I said, regretting that I had not been onto him sooner.

"Stop it! You were smart enough to realize it was Dave who abducted you. See, you're no dummy."

"Oh, come on—it took me way too long to figure that one out. Eventually I realized it had to be Dave. He was the one with the power to call off the dogs from my trail. Also, he was shrewd enough to put on Italian cologne. Not so stupid—made me think it had something to do with Frankie Messina."

"Sneaky bastard. I would have never guessed he had it in him."

"People will blow you away with their dark sides. Every time."

"You and I don't have dark sides, do we?"

"Of course not. We're perfect angels. Saints, actually. Why would you even ask?"

French grinned and gave me a little peck on the cheek and a quick squeeze.

"There was also his scuffed shoe," I said.

"What do you mean?" French asked.

"On the night Frankie was killed, Rick questioned David in his office in front of me. Dave claimed he had been making rounds in the hotel all day and evening, preparing for the big party at Orange 43. I looked down and saw the toe of his right shoe was scuffed. I realized he'd tripped over something in the sculpture garden, as I'd seen him do before. He hadn't only been in the hotel. If he lied about that, then he was covering up his comings and goings that night."

"You're observant, I'll give you that. I still can't believe David would do such a thing. He's not the guy I always thought he was," French said, shaking his head.

"No kidding," I replied. "What about the whopper he told Rick about seeing you near Orange 43 right before the big party?"

"You fell for it at first," French teased.

"Okay, for a while I was in a froth about it. The more I thought it over, the more I realized it was impossible. He had to be making the whole thing up."

"You think?" French asked, giving me a hug, "as if I could be that close to you and not come see you. The whole idea is absurd."

"That was the final piece of the puzzle. That's when I realized he wasn't fishing with tackle. He had gone a little soft in the noodle when no one was looking."

"Just plain nuts," French answered. "That's what I call it. It makes me sick to my stomach to think of the access he had to all of us."

"Awful, isn't it? There's just no telling what a sick mind can justify. He was ambitious. He was tired of his small town life and his small town wife. He found a girl he wanted to impress. He felt entitled to have it all, and he was ready to go to any lengths to get it. He was going to get the girl, the social status and the alpha dog position."

"What a sicko. Margie was next on his list, I'll bet, and you were probably next after that," French said, his face serious.

"I think you may be right," I said.

"Come on," French said. "Drink up and let's take a walk." I slurped up the last drops while he added a tip to our bill and signed it to our room. He took me by the hand and we rose to our feet.

"They make a strong smoothic," I said, a little unsteady. "Tasted so innocent."

"Tastes can be deceiving. When you weren't paying attention, I spoke to our waitress and had her make you a double." He winked at me.

"I know that's a lie and you know I hate people who wink," I said, glad he put his arm around me as he led me back to the street.

A soft breeze was playing through the leaves of the banyan trees. People were walking to cafés, bars, shops, hotels and motels. They were strolling, talking, carrying colorful plastic bags full of souvenirs from Key West.

We stopped in front of a storefront with butcher paper in the windows and a sign that read, "COMING SOON: Silver Threads and Gold Things Needed by Mona Luzi".

"I can't believe it," I said. "Mona is actually launching her own jewelry line, just like she said she would."

"I never thought of her as a businesswoman," French said.

Shadows moved behind the butcher block, so we walked around the side and popped our heads in the back door.

"Oh my gosh, look what the trade winds blew in," Mona said, giving us air hugs and kisses on each cheek.

"What do you think?" she asked, sounding as excited as a little kid.

We walked through the shop, looking at the lighting, the art work on the walls, the display cases filled with her beautiful creations. We told her the shop was going to be a big success.

"I think it'll be a big hit, too," She looked down, her smile shy. "It's only a shame Vacaar isn't here to see it."

"He would be so proud of you," I told her, knowing it was true.

We said our goodbyes and, as we walked down the street, his arm still firmly around my waist, French looked at me and said, "You see, she is a genuine person, after all. And talented, besides."

"She is lovely," I agreed, " and I'd consider her competition, if I thought she were your type."

"You would not," he said, giving me a playful jab in the ribs, "You know damn well she's too tall for me. I like 'em petite and sultry."

I think I blushed. I liked this relaxed and loving French, prone to praise and public displays of affection. I'd have to see to it that he was accused of more murders as our lives unfolded together.

Chapter 62

Two weeks passed since the police hauled David away in their cruiser and Margie ran down the main thoroughfare of Windermere, creating a ruckus all the way to her house on Pine, poor dear. French and I were settling back into our usual routine of four or five business dinners a week. Tonight, we had entertained some Saudi princes at Papa's Place and were happy to be home.

"Did you know some of our VIPs got ripped off earlier today?" French asked, as we undressed for bed.

"No," I said. "I hadn't heard. What happened?"

"Someone broke into the suite while the guests were in it," he said. "They were on the top floor, and the burglars swept through the main floor, making off with the woman's purse, some jewelry on the powder room counter, and a video camera."

"Wow! Can you imagine that? It takes some balls to pull that off."

"No kidding," French said.

"It had to be an inside job, don't you think?" I asked.

"Yes and no," French answered. "We've been hearing some bad things about the employees of the company that makes and installs the swipe locks."

"Uh-oh," I said. "That's a little creepy."

He nodded. After a moment, he said, "We called Rick and Tom immediately, of course. I don't suppose they dropped by to say hello, while they were down here?"

"Not hardly," I answered, taking off my pearl stud earrings and dropping them into the crystal dish on my nightstand.

"Never got a thank you note from them for researching David's family history of mental illness or for solving the murders, either?" he asked.

"Uh, no. The note must have blown off the porch. I don't think the publicity the case got in the *Sentinel* or on the local TV channels helped cement my friendship with Mutt and Jeff, either," I said.

"That's about right," French said. "Still it's a shame. There's too little gratitude in the world today."

"I am crushed by their lack of civility," I offered, as I hopped into bed and snuggled under my down coverlet. I patted his side of the mattress and batted my eyelashes. "Come here, big boy," I said. "I'm going to need some serious comforting and you're just the man for the job."

Chapter 63

Memories of the manager's meeting and all the attendant angst, heartache and craziness were beginning to fade. This summer was the busiest one ever at Silver Pines.

It was a Thursday and French had left for work a while ago. I stretched, got up, walked to the French doors and looked through the bedroom sheers at the lake and the countryside beyond.

The sun was already blazing, as it did every summer morning. I saw clouds gathering on the distant horizon that would later explode into a rumbling fury. The sound and light show began each day around 3:00 p.m., not that it helped. Once the black clouds, thunder, and lightening dissipated, the air was even hotter and steamier than it had been before.

Still, I was happy because I had every reason to be happy. I lived on a stylish resort in Florida. I had a hard man who was good to find. My dear friends, Jake and Lily, were only a phone call away and both French's and my families were only a cross-country flight away in California.

French's brother and sister-in-law wanted to visit us and experience Disney World with their children, Scotty and Ian. We thought their kids were too young to remember the visit once they were adults, but Rob and Cathy would not be dissuaded.

"Okay," French and I told them, "if you insist. We'll be thrilled to see you. We've got lots of things to show you, not just Disney or the other attractions. There's Saint Augustine and Mount Dora, there are country flea markets, antique shows, local crab shacks and juke joints that'll knock your socks off."

They couldn't wait to book their flight.

"There's just one thing," we told them. "Whatever you do, don't come in August. It's hotter than a five alarm chili here in August. Also, there are major thunderstorms every afternoon. They bite into the sightseeing schedule and they're scary as hell. Orlando is overrun with tourists in August and they've all got screaming, overly hot and tired kids, who get nastier and uglier during the course of the day. You'll stand in line for over two hours at the more popular rides, like the Haunted Mansion or Pirates of the Caribbean."

The phone rang. I walked to my nightstand and picked it up. It had to be French.

"Hi, darling," he said. "How's my love this morning?"

"I'm bright-eyed and bushy-tailed," I told him.

"I was just making sure you're up," he said.

"Yes, I know," I answered. "I'm up. Wouldn't miss this for the world," I said, scratching a bump on my midriff.

"That's my girl," he said. "Give them my regards and tell them I'll meet up with you for cocktails tonight after work."

"Of course, honey." I said and blew him a kiss goodbye.

An hour later, I was headed up I-4 and then east on State Route 528, en route to Orlando International Airport. I felt pretty in my new peach linen suit and matching, woven leather sandals. I was picking up my in-laws and nephews and bringing them back with me to the Sapphire Silver Pines Resort.

In the middle of August.

About the Author

Marta Chausée is a prize-winning Southern California author from a cross-cultural background. Her debut novel, Murder's Last Resort, was a winner in the 2012 Dark Oak Mystery contest. She enjoys killing people in her murder mysteries and also writes other fiction, non-fiction, creative non-fiction, and poetry.

When not writing at her desk, she grabs her iPad, jumps on her bike and writes on the road. Most days, you can find her at her favorite haunts along Historic Route 66. She's the one with thought bubbles above her head and a faraway look in her eyes.

She once slept in the luggage rack of a train compartment from Gibraltar to Madrid, but currently lives in a treehouse in an enchanted college town near Los Angeles, with her flying luck dragon, Falcor, and her writer buddies, friends and family nearby.

2589585R00126

Made in the USA
San Bernardino, CA
09 May 2013